ROBERT FORSTER

CROWN LANE

A rural boomer's tale

First published in Great Britain in 2024

Copyright © Robert Forster

The moral right of the author has been asserted.

All rights reserved.

All characters and events in this publication, other than those
clearly in the public domain, are fictitious and any resem-
blance to real persons, living or dead, is purely coincidental.

No part of this publication may be reproduced, stored in a retrieval system,
or transmitted, in any form or by any means, without the prior permission in
writing of the publisher, nor be otherwise circulated in any form of binding or
cover other than that in which it is published and without a similar condition
including this condition being imposed on the subsequent purchaser.

Editing, design, typesetting and publishing by UK Book Publishing.

www.ukbookpublishing.com

ISBN: 978-1-917329-34-7

CROWN LANE

Ben was in a secure place. He was on his back, on a rug, in front of a coal fire, and his mother and grandmother were taking turns to tickle his tummy. Firelight flickered on a poker's brass handle. He flipped himself over and wriggled towards it. Alice caught his ankles and pulled him back.

"Fire, Ben," she warned. "Fire hot. Fire bad."

She was ignored so she picked him up and sat him at her feet.

"No," she said. "Fire. No."

Ben rubbed noses with his Golliwog, played with his toes, heaved himself onto all fours and headed for the poker.

The women looked at each other.

"I'll get a fireguard," said Meg.

Alice sat Ben on her knee. Played with him. Distracted him.

But when she put him down he set off for the poker again.

CHAPTER ONE

Bentcross and Wheelstones

Relief was intense when the fighting stopped. The young men who had survived returned to families pleased they had not been killed and armed German soldiers would not be standing at the end of their street.

But five years of all-out war had wrung Britain dry. Bread had to be rationed, gas and electricity were too, and the winter of 1946/47 was bitter.

People struggled to feed themselves and fought to keep warm. They went to bed wearing overcoats. Sheep's heads were boiled to make soup.

Blizzards blocked railways and roads, destroyed crops and killed livestock. More misery was spread by flood.

Then June's sunlight blazed and the worst was over.

There had been a tidal wave of babies and a National Health Service was launched to protect them.

A torrent of children swamped infant schools. Out of class they chased each other over open fields or through vehicle-free streets.

Food rationing was scrapped. Classrooms in junior schools began to bulge too, living standards continued to rise, and embedded class-based restraints on social mobility began to ease.

Morwick, described by many as a pleasant Pennine town, rolled over several slopes. At their base, beside Fullers Burn, old houses, often tiny, and always crowded, were crammed between glass ovens, a fellmonger, a foundry, and a coking plant.

Bentcross, and similar streets with four-roomed homes, stood halfway. Sports fields, public parks, a castle, a livestock market, and a grammar school mixed in. Above them houses became progressively detached, also much larger, until on top, well away from dirt, noise, neighbours or smell, a handful of mansions could preen. Within Morwick class status was defined by residential location. Elevation could not have been more clearly underlined.

Scott and Alice Robson lived on Bentcross. He had been a sergeant when he'd taken a bullet through a lung in North Africa and had served as a weapons instructor until he was de-mobbed. He could no longer work on farms so became a post office supervisor instead.

Alice's parents farmed Wheelstones where Old Kit hand-milked eight cows and Meg churned butter which, apart from an occasional bullock and something like forty fat lambs each autumn, seemed to be the only thing they sold. Their lifestyle was unusually self-sufficient, painstakingly careful and Methodist Chapel discreet.

A child's memory is fitful. Ben had heard Meg say goodnight before her door latch clicked and they stood in darkness. He had held his mother's hand as they crossed moonlit cobbles then waited, breath pluming, at the farm gate for Billy Milburn to pull up with his bus.

The rime on Morwick's pavements had twinkled as Alice, shoulders back to balance her belly, towed him through its streets. She slipped as they passed the War Memorial and crashed on her back. Shadowed adults had buzzed like flies. Loud voices made no sense. Someone who knew his name had rested their hand on his shoulder. A man kneeling beside Alice kept asking if she was all-right.

Then, wearing a strange nightgown and lying in a strange bed, she had pointed to a green box.

"Your sister's in there."

He stood on tiptoe. She was pink, wrinkled and surrounded by tubes. His fingers scrabbled against the incubator's lid.

***

Bentcross was a wide street and there were no parked cars.

Noisy boys with short trousers and scabby knees played tag. Sisters, all in frocks, most holding dolls, sat on its kerbs in groups.

Mothers enjoying a warm May evening lingered at their front doors.

"Don't trip over," warned one.

Others, wearing bibbed pinafores and head scarves tied like turbans, made plans to celebrate Princess Elizabeth's Coronation.

"Bedtime soon," called Alice.

Other mothers joined in.

"Hurry up now."

"In you go."

The road began to empty.

She smiled when Ben came in through the backyard.

"Let me see your shoes."

Satisfied he had not carried in dog shit, she sat him on the sink top, ran some hot water, soaped a flannel, and washed his legs.

"Now this," she said, filling a teaspoon with government issue cod liver oil. He grimaced.

"Orange juice to take away the taste then wash your hands and face and get ready for bed."

"Where's Catherine?"

"Where you should be."

"Read me a story first."

There was a knock at the back door.

Scott put down his crossword.

"It'll be Jenny," he said.

Jenny, who lived directly opposite, was still excited next day. A string of red, white, and blue rags hung from her upstairs window. It joined a coil that lay at her slippered feet. She tied its looped end to a clothes prop, hoisted it high, and marched, a pinafored standard bearer, across the road to the upstairs window where Alice, arm outstretched, was leaning.

"Got it," she said and began to haul it in.

Jenny scanned the crisscross skeins of bunting that already lined the street.

"Aren't they marvellous."

Ben went to school in a jumper with the Coronation Coach knitted into it. Catherine twisted endless strings of red, white and blue wool which she fumbled into clumsy bows.

Only television was black and white. Jenny's husband had come home with Bentcross's first and their living room was crowded. Children, running in and out, tried to make sense of its tiny screen. "Has she been crowned yet?" asked Barbara Fenwick for the umpteenth time.

A line of trestle tables had filled the street. Some places had been set.

Then it rained.

Excited children, running ahead of their parents, poured into the Castle Institute where, careless of the chaos they created, they sat next to others they did not know and ate sandwiches made by mothers from the other side of town.

There were more surprises when a bath, huge, white, and heavy, appeared in the Robsons' backyard.

There had been dust and destruction then more flat capped men in overalls lugging wrenches and bending copper pipes.

Now he and Catherine were sitting in it, warm water swished navel high, and Alice was washing their hair.

"Two rules," she said. "No splashing and I'm the only one who can turn on the hot tap."

Ben was determined to take his new mask to school. It had been cut from the back of a breakfast cereal packet.

Its black face was crowned with a feather headdress and a bone had been pushed through its nose.

Alice was uncertain.

Scott had said no.

So he'd hidden it in the backyard.

"I'm King of the Jungle," he shouted when he ran into the playground.

Children crowded him, laughing.

He pushed his masked face towards them and made fierce noises.

"What's going on?" shouted Miss Chatham. "Stop this dreadful racket."

"You," she said, stabbing her finger. "Give me that silly thing. And get over there."

Conformity was King.

Ben, head down, slunk towards an empty corner.

Cissie Lish joined him. She was from deepest Fullers Burn.

Scruffy, red nosed, and underfed, she, and her family, sat foursquare on Morwick's lowest social rung.

Her mother, who always dressed in old fashioned black, and wrinkled woollen stockings, looked little different than she would have done at any time in the town's poverty-filled past.

The last time he had seen them, Mrs Lish was being scolded for spreading rumours by a mother who lived up the hill.

"It wasn't me, Missus," she'd protested. It may not have been but those who lived at the bottom were used to being kicked.

Cissie had been clinging, shamed and protective, to her mother's heavy skirt.

He'd caught her eye and could see she knew what was happening. She may have been young but she'd already had enough.

She wiped her nose on her sleeve as she came over.

"She's a bad'un that," she said, tipping her chin towards Miss Chatham. "Proper cow. Hits me head with 'er scissors if 'm late for class."

"Let me look at you," said Alice.

He stood at attention while she adjusted his collar, straightened his tie, checked that his shoes had been polished and patted his cheek. It was the signal to go.

"Look after Catherine," she called after him.

Scott came in from the living room as soon as the front door slammed.

He put his arm round Alice's waist.

"Sunday School's such a blessing," he whispered as he led her upstairs.

Ben and Catherine walked up the street, through the nick, and into Bondgate. Other children, equally neat, were streaming towards the Chapel too.

Mrs Stout led the prayers.

Miss Merryweather read a bible story.

The children crayoned in pictures of the Feeding of the Five Thousand.

Then prayed to God to keep them good and ran home.

****

He stood with a cluster of boys watching Sand Martins as they swirled on the opposite bank of a noisy river. Some birds flapped into burrows.

"They hide eggs in those holes," said one.

"Let's have a look," said another.

The Morton was wide. The group hesitated.

"Come on," said Ben. "Let's go."

Mid-stream was difficult but they fought through.

Their arms were too short to reach anything. Then, fed up with skimming stones, they braced themselves to go back.

Alan Johnson slipped, found his feet, and began to whimper. Group confidence evaporated as water pressed against their waists.

Some big boys from Leamside waded in and hauled them out.

Mrs Johnson was standing, arms folded, when Scott answered the front door. When he came back Ben was forced over a chair arm, belted, and sent to bed without supper.

Wheelstones was different. Its sixty-acre kingdom belonged only to them. Meg took Catherine with her when she was hunting for hen's eggs, Ben went with Kit when he shot rabbits on the haugh, and Nanny, the yellow-eyed house goat, followed everyone like a dog. There were rules. The lid on the water butt by the back door had to be put back each time a jug, or pail, was filled; and the bull pen was out of bounds. Ben chattered while Kit milked his cows. Catherine built a Wendy House in a corner of the cart shed. And both were told to stand well back when

Kit was setting gin-traps for rats. "If you touch one, you'll lose your fingers," he warned.

Tom appeared when Ben was moving through Junior School. Alice was standing at their front door when he and his sister came home for dinner. She showed them a bundle in a blanket. His face was less wrinkled, not as pinched, as Catherine's had been.

They took turns to hold him then Alice changed his nappy.

Catherine giggled. "He really is a boy."

Girls did better in class. Their printing was neat, when they crayoned they were careful not to cross lines, they did not shout out answers before being asked, and most got better marks.

Ben had been told not to smudge wet paint but found the blurring attractive. He thought he'd created an orange and green masterpiece.

Miss Temple was furious. The orthodoxy she imposed on everything had been offended. She hauled him to the front, held up his offering and mocked it.

Then, because he did not look sufficiently contrite, produced her drumstick.

"Hold out your right hand."

She hit him three times across his fingers.

It was not the pain that shocked him. It was the viciousness in her eyes.

Girls were more agile than boys too. On sunny days they tucked their dresses into their knickers and practised handstands. Some boys could stand on their hands but none were as supple.

A road sweeper hovered next to them. Still young, and with a writhing smile, he offered to give them a ride on his bin barrow.

"You can cut that out," frowned Mrs Simpson who was watching from her front door.

A bank of scruffy trees stood at the end of Bentcross. They screened a slope still known as The Common where big boys went to smoke and their little brothers built camps. The latest construction was hidden inside a sprawling laurel where deep shadows offered opportunities for secrecy and invention.

Ben was not surprised to hear voices as he ducked under branches towards it. Then stopped in shock. Road Sweeper was there with Catherine and his penis, angry and shockingly thick, was throbbing.

"Touch it. Just touch it," he pleaded.

Catherine shook her head.

Ben stepped out and stood beside her.

"He asked me to show him the camp," she whispered.

"I'll not tell anybody," he promised, as he put his arm across her shoulders.

Nor did he, but Road Sweeper was not seen again.

The sweetshop at the end of Bentcross was always busy. Some kids sucked on Mrs Mills' sherbet liquorice sticks. Others pushed over a threepenny bit and pocketed a tube of fruit gums. A handful had saved enough coins to buy their monthly bottle of lemonade. Other children carrying satchels and wearing an assortment of badged blazers called in on their way home from the railway station. Most bought a sixpenny bar of chocolate. Some came out with more.

The same boys dominated summer evening cricket that was played on the fringes of the nearby club pitch. They had the best bats, best balls and loudest voices. Most of those from Bentcross walked to a public playing field where they improvised cricket, or football, with kids who had come up from Fullers Burn instead.

Shocks, even pleasant ones, arrive without warning.

"We're moving," announced Alice. "We've got the Post Office at Whiteside."

Ben could see she was excited.

One of her brothers farmed at nearby Sunny Banks.

The village was six miles from Morwick so Scott bought a secondhand Ford Prefect. It had four doors. The chrome that fringed the radiator grille was dazzling. Its smooth bonnet was immense.

Bentcross children swarmed unbelievingly to see it.

"My dad's going to buy a Jaguar," said Fatty Old.

They moved that August.

Their detached house had three bedrooms and each child had their own bed.

CHAPTER TWO

Whiteside and Sunny Banks

A world map hung above the Schoolmaster's desk. Ben thought the west end of the Mediterranean looked like a dog's head. It was the Balearics that gave it an eye. Sun poured through the classroom's windows. Wilf Waverley's red heifers were chewing their cud behind the playground fence. Beyond Countess Wood both Wenside and Bleanwick were smudged humps.

Boys and girls sat in age defined groups. Those in the youngest huddle were ten. The oldest, almost thirteen, would soon sit through their final two years at Morwick's new secondary school. Whiteside's parish juniors fidgeted next door. Its infants chattered in an extension.

Long John, the nickname unavoidable because he was a lanky man, asked everyone who came off a farm to confirm their father's acreage, list his cattle by breed, and check if he grew any corn.

Edward Kerr's elbow poked Ben's ribs. His family's holding was Earthly Mires.

"Tommy Tyson's dad's got just ten cows. We've got fifteen."

Ben dropped his head so he could hide his mouth.

"Sunny Banks has twenty. British Friesians. Not mixed breed mongrels like yours."

They stiffened to attention because they'd been spotted.

"I want you to work out the average acreage of Whiteside's farms, the average size of its dairy herds and which breeds of cow are the most common," Long John told his class.

His pupils thought this was much more interesting than arithmetic that hammered on about green bottles or mud pies.

Totty Farr rang the home-time bell and everyone piled out. A handful of Fords and Austins collected the children who had farthest to go. The Hogarths from The Wry wanted Ben to play football but he shook his head, went home, changed into overalls, and climbed a fence instead.

Sunny Banks was a mile away. The bell on St John's struck four times as he walked through Church Close. After he'd crossed The Hawes he sat on a gate. A skylark danced above him and a chainsaw whined in distant woods. He searched to see if his uncle was working in one of his fields. A hare got up as he cut across Roughside. He stopped to see which way it would turn, then climbed the fence into Quarry Edge, dropped down a steep slope, moved through the Home Field, past a steaming muck midden, and into the yard.

His Uncle Bill, a lean man with stubble on his chin, stepped out of a byre.

"Jim's not here. I need a hand."

A heifer, the last of her batch to calve, was standing in a lonely stall. Her back was arched, she'd lifted her tail and her vulva dribbled.

"She's having it difficult. Let's see if you can tell me why."

Ben rolled up his right sleeve and slowly pushed his arm inside her. It was hot, elastic, and dark. His shoulder moved in time with his hand.

"Can you feel both front feet?"

"Yes."

"Where's the head?"

His arm sank deeper.

"Be careful in there. Is it between the legs?"

Ben nodded.

"What do you make of it?"

"It's big?"

Bill Henderson grunted.

"It's enormous."

He took some plaited twine in one hand, pushed in the other, and began to pull. The heifer groaned. Two pale hooves appeared. When the front feet stood out like sticks he tied them together and gave the rope to Ben.

"Pull down while I ease the head."

He took it two-handed.

"Downwards. Always downwards. Towards her back feet."

He strained. The rope was taking just about all his weight. The calf's head appeared. Then its shoulders. It fell to the floor, in a rush of fluid, and with a wet slap. The heifer quivered then stood unmoving with staring eyes.

He was told to clean the calf's nostrils, then its mouth, and shake its shoulder. It began to struggle and tried to lift its head. He untied the twine and stepped back.

"What is it?"

He lifted the calf's hind leg. No ball bag.

"Heifer."

Edward Kerr was waiting next time school ended.

"Let's give Stotts Beck another go."

The stream was running slowly. Its pools were smooth. The early autumn leaves which dotted them were still. Trout waved their tails gently as they rested in shadowed sections beneath a bank. Circular ripple spreads showed where others were rising to midges or flies.

The boys waited. A shadow flicked. Ben pointed.

"Too small," Edward said.

"There," said Ben, pointing again.

He rolled up his overalls and waded in. The trout thought it was safe under its stone until Ben, his forefinger deep in one of its gills and thumb fixed in the other, hauled it out.

Edward, also up to his knees, caught one in the next pool.

Another fish was threaded onto their hazel switch after the boys had moved upstream.

Scott called him back into the kitchen after tea. Alice was sitting beside him. He pointed to one of the chairs.

"You'll soon be taking your Eleven-Plus."

It was not a question.

"The Schoolmaster thinks you could pass."

If he did it meant Grammar School in Morwick and one of those silly badged caps.

"You have to take it seriously," said Alice.

He was silent.

"What do you think?"

He knew better than to shrug.

His parents looked at each other.

"You've got to give yourself a chance," said Alice.

"I want work on a farm."

"If you do well at Grammar School you could go to university."

"You would learn more about the world than you ever could at home."

***

Jim Henderson let the steering wheel spin as the tractor slid through winter mud in a rutted gate. Ben rode its drawbar. His balance was already practised. Lines of turnips stood ready to be lifted. He stepped down, grabbed a stem of leaves, and pulled the first one out.

"Keep at it. I'll load them," said Jim.

A rhythm was established as they settled to their task.

His cousin encouraged him.

"They're easier to throw off than they are to throw on," he said.

Hungry heifers crowded the trailer as soon as it came into their field. But the bull they were running with was hostile. The pasture was Duke's fiefdom. The trailer was threatening his territory. The heifers were his herd. He stalked it, pawed the ground, snorted, then knelt to rip up turf with his horns.

When Ben began to throw out turnips, Duke put his head under its rear end and heaved. His neck was huge. He almost lifted a wheel.

"Keep as far away as you can," called Jim.

The bull, head swinging and hooves plunging, moved from one side of the load to the other.

"Hold tight," said Jim when, feeding finished, he opened the throttle and headed for the gate.

The bull did not follow.

"What's got into him?" asked Ben.

Jim frowned. "He'll settle down when he knows it's routine."

The Chapel's Sunday School ripped an hour out of the rest of the weekend. Boys from Whiteside's non-conformist families chafed in shirts and ties. The girls, some in embroidered blouses, and all wearing carefully polished shoes, were even neater. Geordie Elliott, moustache bristling and bald patch shining, pounded relentless mis-chords on the organ. Jack Graham, the superintendent, invited them to sink their heads in prayer and thanked God for a lovely sunny day. Ben wriggled in his seat. Edward Kerr had found an overhang beside Foulshaw Burn and was building a new den.

Monday meant school and Long John's spectacles were gleaming. Freshly drawn graphs lined his classroom's wall. Exercise books were open and each pupil's head was up.

"I want you to summarise the survey then show it to your parents when you get home."

"What is the average size of a Whiteside farm?"

"Sixty-four acres."

"How many have a dairy herd?"

"Ninety-four per cent."

"How many cows are in the average herd?"

"Twelve."

Long John nodded.

"What else does the survey tell us?"

This time pupil reaction was a blank stare.

"A mixed farm with twelve dairy cows earns enough to support a family."

The Schoolmaster waited for this to sink in.

"How many of your fathers have a car?"

There was a big show of hands.

"My dad's getting a Hillman Minx."

"Have you seen Laidlaw's Riley?"

Heads turned. A Riley! Billy Laidlaw had three farms. Even so. A Riley!

Some shocks are unpleasant.

"Grandad's retiring," Alice told the meal table.

Eating stopped.

"Where are they going to live?" said Scott.

Catherine looked at everyone in turn.

"I'm going over to see them," said Ben.

Wicket gates and a line of stiles took him through Syke Wood. A wood pigeon clattered off. A jay scolded. Ned Johnson was opening out a stand of young pine. He stopped as Ben walked towards him, leaned on his G-bar and pointed to a hollow in the grass.

"I'd say a deer lay up there last night."

After he left the trees he could see his grandfather's sheep were on Bolisher. Smoke was lifting from Wheelstones' chimney. The grass on Middle Paisley was thin and yellow. If it had been summer it would have carried a carpet of flowers and he would have picked some Lady's Smock.

Kit was washing Punch's legs. Smoke from a full strength Craven "A" sieved his moustache. Meg's clogs clattered as she hurried to put an arm across his shoulders. Nanny stared at him with yellow eyes.

"I'll just give him his feed," said Kit as he led the Shire into the stable.

Meg had been churning butter. He turned the paddles while she boiled the kettle. Currant scones and butterfly cakes thumped onto the table. Kit sat down too.

"It'd be Alice who told you?"

His grandmother began churning again. Flecks of yellow told him the slosh was beginning to quicken.

"We'll sell up in spring," Kit said.

Bill Henderson and Gladys sat opposite each other in easy chairs at Sunny Banks.

They would take over Wheelstones after the sale.

Gladys looked up from her knitting.

"You're sure your mam and dad don't want to leave the house?"

Henderson puffed out pipe smoke.

"I am."

"Good. They'll keep an eye on things."

***

Just four pupils were sitting at their desks. The Eleven-Plus had stalked them for years. Now they would have to confront it.

A teacher from another village faced them.

"You must use the pencils you have been given – not pens. You have forty-five minutes to answer the first set of questions. Don't turn the paper over until I tell you. There'll be a short break before you start the second."

Edward Kerr rolled his eyes.

Ben tried not to be distracted.

Foxhounds, tan, white, black and brindle, delivered almost immediate relief. They arrived in a flood of inquisitive noses and flailing rear ends, as they poured down a wagon ramp and inspected the people who had gathered to greet them. A man astride a glossy bay cracked a whip and called them to order.

"Look at their tails," he said.

"Sterns," corrected his grandfather.

The man on a huge chestnut tooted some notes on a horn.

"Right," said Kit, hurrying towards his van. "Time to go."

Huntley Vale lay below them. Hounds were scouring Shipley Whins. A tan bitch whimpered. A liver and white dog joined her. Kit pointed to a dark streak running a straight line downhill. The rider on the chestnut blew urgently. Hounds spread themselves over the fox's trail. Horses, all shapes and sizes, followed. The front runners were hoisting themselves over a line of fences.

"Would you like to do that?" Kit asked.

Whiteside's parishioners celebrated Christmas with unusually full plates. Memories of wartime rationing had still to be banished and it pleased them to watch their children eating as much as they could. The Women's Institute always put on a good feed. Sandwiches, very few with plain jam and some with ham, even tinned salmon, were first onto the Parish Hall's trestle tables. Then cheese scones, drop scones and savoury flans. Butterfly cakes, fruit cake, marshmallows in red tin foil, and chocolate biscuits followed. The finale was Battenburg and Christmas Cake.

Tea at the Methodist Chapel's social was even better. The meat in the sandwiches was thicker and then there were games. Boys and girls stood alternately for the balloon relay. Hands were forbidden to help the uncooperative globs squeak the length of each line. This could only be done by careful transfer from beneath one chin to the security of the equally tight grip offered by another. Cheeks inevitably rubbed together.

"Like horses necking," said Edward.

Jolly Bachelor topped it. Methodists were fierce in their condemnation of the demon drink but did nothing to discourage inter-sex affection, so a circle was formed which surrounded a single girl or boy, then everyone, including their mothers, held hands and sang:

"One jolly bachelor all alone
Nothing to do but mind his home
He looked to the East and then to the West
He chose the one that he loved best."

After selection each couple stood in the middle and kissed. Carol Atkinson, a year younger than him, had soft lips. Ben picked her out as often as he dared. Carol must have liked the touch of his lips too. She almost always chose him when it was her turn. Matrons, some with impressive chin hair, swapped knowing glances.

He was at Sunny Banks with his Uncle Bill when an east wind began to whip in heavy blasts of snow.

Henderson had watched the sky all morning.

A blizzard was howling when they settled down to dinner.

"We'll have to get the sheep in. Jim, you make space in the hayshed."

He looked at Ben. "Let's get you properly dressed."

Gladys gave him a khaki balaclava. "Tuck both ends inside your jacket. Now get into this."

"This" was an old duffel coat.

"Wear your overalls outside your wellies. And don't lose these."

"These" were a thick pair of gloves.

Henderson, huge in an army greatcoat, gave him a stick. "It's filling the lane. We'll cut through Rough Strothers and bring them back round Blue Hill. Walk behind me. Don't stop."

He felt clumsy in his heavy clothes. Curtains of snow stung his face. Fly, the collie, had her head down too.

The ewes, fleeces iced and heavy, were huddled in a field corner. Henderson's face was purple. His nose dripped. The wind was keening. He had to shout to make himself heard.

"Keep them bunched up. Watch out for stragglers. Fly'll keep them away from the dyke backs."

The trudge back had been difficult. Snow in some hollows was already deeper than his knees. And awkward ewes had to be chased to stop them running back. His face was numb, and his legs were aching, so the final push through the yard gate was a relief. His uncle was counting heads.

"They're all here. You'd better get in the house."

"Ben's a snowman," said Catherine after a tractor had taken him home.

Alice handed him a neatly wrapped parcel.

"Master Ben Robson," it said.

It was oblong. Its outline smooth.

"From Auntie Kathleen. Because you're going to Grammar School."

It was Rudyard Kipling's The Jungle Book.

His Auntie Doris posted King Solomon's Mines.

A sow's litter was about to be weaned. The male piglets castrated.

He held them up by the hind legs while Henderson slashed their scrotum with a razor, squeezed out each testicle, cut the connecting cord and dropped them on the pen's cement floor.

There was very little blood.

The piglets, now hogs, no longer boars, seemed unaffected.

Some nuzzled at their discarded, bean-shaped, stones.

"It's got to be done," said Henderson as Ben, knees bent, hands hunting, grabbed another.

The cuts were typically precise. Both testicles were removed.

But when the piglet was put down a fan shaped coil of wet intestine slipped slowly out.

The damage was wrenchingly fundamental. The most horrifying thing he'd seen.

Henderson cursed. "Must have a rupture."

Another coil appeared. It hung, with grotesque precision, exactly alongside the first.

"We'll have to kill it."

He came back from the tool shed with a hammer and spiked bolt.

Ben held the piglet down.

Henderson positioned the spike and swung.

The boy was shaken. He had felt the piglet die.

He was given the kidneys after the carcase had been disembowelled.

They were fried for his breakfast next morning.

"Mary Dodd sent me these," said Alice pointing to the kitchen table. "Bobby's grown out of them. If they don't fit, I'll buy new ones."

He saw the cap first. The black blazer had a badge as well. Words that could only be Latin were strung across a flame crested shield.

"Try it on," his mother prompted.

He submitted as she excitedly tugged its sleeves, fussed with the collar and pulled at the back.

"How does it feel?"

He wanted to say "awkward" but grunted instead. She laughed when he put on his cap.

"There's rugby shirts, the socks and your PT strip. You'll have to wear short trousers for the first year. They're strict about that. I'll buy new ones. And a pullover. Will you be able to wear your brown shoes? You'll need a haversack to carry your books."

Education was a village effort.

Malcom Findlay's dad picked up swill from the school's kitchen for his pigs.

And one afternoon he dropped off a dead badger.

It was the first the children had seen. An old boar with a mangled throat.

The carcase was weighed and measured. Sketches underlined its long teeth, coarse hair and short legs.

Long John was especially interested in its heavily clawed forepaws.

"They are a specialist digging tool. Designed to make it easier to get to roots and grubs. Useful when extending its sett as well."

The stack yard at Wheelstones was crowded. Well-used tools, each carrying a number, lay in rows. Other equipment, everything from the horse drawn hay rake to a one-furrow plough, was lined up too. Meg and Kit were cashing their pension. Expectant farmers, more people than Ben knew, had made a circle around the byre door. A nervous Shorthorn, head down and udder swinging, was prodded forward. A chanting auctioneer hunted for bids. He cracked a stick against his gaiters. A gap opened to let her out. The next cow was immediately nudged in. Wagons stood ready to take them away. He knew his grandparents' life had to be hacked back but had not expected the process to be as ruthless. When Punch, a head and neck taller than the men surrounding him, was led in to be sold, he found Catherine and they backed away.

A gleaming fertiliser spreader, as unfamiliar as a spaceship, stood in front of the cart shed at Sunny Banks. Its bin was smooth, concave and deep.

"It'll hold four hundredweight," said Jim. "Got a twelve-foot spread."

Bill Henderson turned to Ben.

"We'll be able to grow grass well into autumn. If we dress pastures in March we could turn the cows out earlier."

He spun two discs at the base of the inverted cone.

"They'll cover some ground. When I was your age we had to throw out artificial by hand."

"It's delivered in hundredweight bags. No more shovelling up from heaps of slag or lime," said Jim.

Ben remembered one of Long John's lessons.

"Does artificial have phosphate, nitrogen and potash?"

"All three. Equal amounts. It'll help to feed the soil. It's balanced," his uncle replied.

Nanny's yellow eyes still stared. The bindweed Ben had crushed crossing the cobbles was aromatic. His grandmother had been baking. She took his arm and steered him into the yard. Her clogs clattered. There was flour on his sleeve.

"You're going to like this."

Kit joined them at the stable door. He pointed at Punch's loose box. Ben stood on tiptoe to peer in. The pony was roan. It stepped forward and snuffed his hands.

"Whose is he?"

"He's been hunted. He's yours."

"What's he called?"

"Josh."

CHAPTER THREE

Julia Corneliam Amat

There were more people in the Grammar School's main hall than he had seen in one place before. Rank after rank of progressively older pupils had filed past. The acne attacks on some faces looked painful. Stiff white shirts and uniform ties could not hide the maturity of the senior girls. Some boys had fussy hairstyles. Others had cultivated a truculent slouch. A couple had to shave their chins.

"Prefects have a green stripe above their badge," whispered a blond boy.

Gowned teachers, male and female, old and young, sat stiffly on the stage above them. The headmaster confirmed a number and everyone shuffled through a hymn. The Head Boy, his quiff perfect, brylcreem glistening, and parting ruler straight, was confident when he read the lesson. Blond Boy was whispering again.

"That's Julian Burton. His dad's a surgeon. They live on Crown Lane."

Crown Lane! The Morwick boys who were listening were automatically impressed.

Back in their classroom IA's Form Master was hitching his gown.

"Listen carefully.

"You are privileged. You have passed your Eleven-plus which means that in intelligence capacity terms you sit within Britain's top five per cent. You are your country's future. It is your duty, bounden duty, to work hard and be successful. At all times you must remember that.

"You are also the school's first co-education year. Boys and girls in the same class. You will be familiar with this from junior school, but older pupils will find it strange.

"We have strict rules. You must always walk on the left-hand side of the corridor, you must hand your homework in on time, and you must not talk in class. Your timetable is on the notice board. You should make copies. Your first lesson is Latin. It begins at 9.20. There are eight 40-minute lessons each day. A bell will ring at the end of each one."

"Julia Corneliam amat," declared Mr Braithwaite. "It's an appropriate sentence because this is the first time I have taught girls."

His gown swished as he turned to chalk out the present tense declension of the Latin verb to love. Group bewilderment hung like mist.

"Julia is the subject of the sentence. The verb amat is in accusative form. It confirms Julia's love is directed at a second person or object. The a-m suffix attached to Cornelia is also accusative. The link, the two accusatives, confirm Cornelia is the object of Julia's love."

Braithwaite smiled at the girl sitting nearest to him then pointed to the boy beside her.

"Please translate Julia Corneliam amat."

His head dropped. A puddle spread. He had pissed himself. Ben, who had found a less conspicuous seat, was sympathetic.

The bus station was a scrum. Getting on the Whiteside bus was too. Bobby Dodd, immeasurably his senior because he had Fourth Form status, shepherded him into a front seat.

"Keep away from the back until you're older," he warned.

Ben risked a peep. Big boys, fifteen-year-olds from different villages, were locked in a tangle of wrestling arms and shouting heads.

"What are you looking at?" bellowed a curly haired giant.

He ducked quickly back.

"See if your Uncle Bill'll let you have his .22?" said Edward Kerr.

"Dene Bank's crawling with rabbits. I'll bring a .410."

"Meet you at Lane End after tea."

The boys lifted their heads over the lip of a hill. A score of rabbits were feeding below them.

"I'll go for the one that's closest," Ben whispered.

"I'll blast when they run for cover," said Edward.

Ben made himself comfortable, pushed in a round, closed the breech, released the safety catch, picked his target, set himself to aim straight, and fired. The doe was knocked flat, kicked a little, then died.

Edward had shot a rabbit too. He tossed it down and pulled out one of his father's cigarettes. He and Ben lay back and studied the sky. An occasional sheep bleated. Noisy geese flew overhead.

"Better than school?" said Edward.

"Anything'd be better than amo, amas, amat."

Edward frowned.

"What the hell is that?"

Morwick's castle keep stood proud. A heather moor, still purple, topped the valley slope beyond. Gulls were feeding at one end of the sport's pitches that separated two schools. A group of girls left the low, brick built, Secondary Modern and began to play rounders. The Grammar School frowned on the opposite side. Its bell tower and mullioned windows stood high. Within its dressed stone walls, Ben's class was being introduced to algebra.

His brain had fogged as he struggled with X+Y. Blond Boy had tried to help but Ben's whispering had jarred a Mr Purvis nerve.

"Come to the front," the teacher ordered. "Your choice. Write 'I must not talk in class' one hundred times or three strokes with the slipper?"

"Slipper, sir."

It was quick. The writing would take time. He watched as a gym shoe was taken from a briefcase. It must have been size twelve.

Hugh Walker was gloatingly miming strokes. Other boys were grinning. Most girls were apprehensive. He bent over. Purvis stepped back.

Whack.

He absorbed it.

Whack.

He absorbed that too.

"Last one," said Purvis.

Whack.

He straightened up. He kept his face expressionless.

"Don't talk in my class again."

"Village boy," mocked Judy Clark as he passed her desk.

She lived near Crown Lane so was licensed to be snobby.

Josh clattered into the yard at Earthly Mires where the Kerrs were waiting.

"What's he like loading?" called Alf.

"Soon find out," said Edward as Ben swung down.

A big bay gelding stood in the back of the wagon.

Edward's piebald was beside him.

Josh thumped up the ramp and Alf tied him in.

"He's done that before."

They unloaded at Shipton where the Morvales' hounds stood with forty riders.

"Stay right behind me," said Alf as the hunt moved off.

Josh was excited. There was froth in his nostrils, sweat across his chest and on his withers, and he had lifted his tail.

Edward's pony was seasoned but still arched its neck and held its head high.

They trotted along a lane and stopped by Thrimble Wood. Riders waited as the hounds combed through. Some horses stood to attention with their ears pricked. Others cropped grass and occasionally lifted their heads to listen.

A horn sounded and Field Master pushed on.

"Nothing doing," said Alf as they fell into line.

They were on a road now, bumping along in a fast trot, to the next cover.

They watched the whipper-in take position as the hounds nosed through a thick rank of rushes.

"He's seen him," said Alf swinging his bay round.

"Try to keep up. If things get going, hang on."

The whipper-in, standing in his stirrups, was holding his arm along a line that pointed to Brigg End.

Field Master led the way. Ben and Edward tucked in.

The front runners were already over the first fence.

"Bridge your reins and follow me," ordered Alf, squeezing his knees.

His horse flew over.

Edward, eyes concentrated, brow furrowed, tracked him.

Ben did exactly what he'd been told.

He held Josh's head straight, clamped his knees just before take-off, and sailed over too.

"That was good," said Alf who'd peeled off to watch.

"Stay with him like that and you'll be fine."

They rode fast and hard for ten minutes then reined in.

The hounds had checked. They'd lost the fox. Both boys were laughing.

Their pony's enthusiasm, and the strange mid-jump silence when both horse and rider hung in the air, had lifted them.

Field Master trotted up.

"Enjoy that?"

They nodded their heads at the same time.

Each Christmas Eve carol singers from Whiteside's Methodist Chapel reinforced community good will and harvested its maintenance money.

Every house in the village was sung to, its door knocker banged, and a collection box rattled.

Ben was among the youngsters who climbed into the back of half-a-dozen cars which set off to sing to the gentry.

Whiteside Hall was the first stop.

"We'll start with While Shepherds Watched," said Geordie Elliott.

A uniformed maid opened the front door when they'd finished.

The carpeted corridor was endless. A parade of pictures which concentrated on formal flowered gardens and foxhunting lined its walls.

They shuffled into a pillared reception area where two couples, each in evening dress, watched from elegantly curved stairs.

Deep inside the room smoke curled from a cigar held in a languid hand.

Nothing more could be seen because the man attached to the hand was hidden by the back of his chair.

"Away in a Manger," whispered Jack Graham.

The hand's forefinger occasionally tapped off ash as they sang.

The Superintendent coughed to confirm they'd finished, and the chair swung round.

Colonel Leighton, grey haired, pink, and plump was benign.

"Marvellous," he said. "Quite marvellous."

His staircase guests beamed patrician agreement.

Colonel Leighton leaned back and waited for more.

Jack Graham caught Gordon Wilson's eye. He stepped forward, a fine tenor, and sang "Silent Night".

His voice resonated perfectly within the room.

Leighton signalled to a line of waiting staff, each holding a tray of glasses with decanters of port or ginger wine.

"They're the same colour," whispered Edward Kerr.

Leighton handed Jack Graham, a confirmed teetotaller who had long ago adopted the Methodist no-alcohol pledge, some ginger wine. They toasted each other, then Leighton palmed something over and the Chapel Superintendent respectfully shook his hand.

Edward took a glass of port when the tray reached him. The maid pretended not to notice so Ben did the same.

Next stop was Major Denton. His wife's welcome was enthusiastic.

"Come in. Come in," she cried. Bosom visibly heaving. Dress a-glitter.

Shooting trophies lined the walls.

"That's the latest. Kenyan plain," she boasted, waving a suntanned arm.

The Chapel folk were dutifully impressed.

Carols were sung and Mrs Denton served the drinks herself.

She winked when she poured crème de menthe for Ben and Edward instead of green ginger.

"We had to bring him back," explained Geordie Elliott. "He's not very well."

Scott expressed his appreciation.

Alice suppressed a disbelieving giggle.

"He's drunk," she snorted as she pushed him hurriedly upstairs.

Boys in blazers stood on one side of the sports pitches that separated the schools. Boys who were not wearing blazers lined the other. Snowballs fell uselessly in the gap between. Each side moved closer. Direct hits were scored.

"Scrub the big mouth," a boy from Belton ordered.

Someone wearing a blazer was hauled down. Snowballs were rubbed in his face. Others were stuffed down his shirt collar. A teacher ran in waving each side back.

Stiff fingers flicked up the back of Ben's neck. His cap was tipped into bus station slush at his feet. The boy from Belton was grinning.

"Don't think we didn't see you."

Bobby Dodd stood next to him.

"Keep it in your pocket. Daft to wear it down here."

Catherine and Gladys came into the yard at Sunny Banks just as Jim led out Duke to serve an in-season cow.

"She's too young for this," said Henderson who was holding the third-calver's head.

But Duke was in action before Gladys could grab Catherine's hand and go.

He didn't need to sniff the cow's pungent vulva.

His penis, a two foot dagger, was already flicking in anticipation.

It vanished as he mounted her without breaking stride.

His eyes bulged as, back arched and hind legs scrabbling, he thrust heavily, before sliding slowly back down.

"That was quick," said Catherine.

Gladys shrugged when she met her husband's eye.

Almost a dozen children, eyes fixed on a silver screen, were spread over a Whiteside living room's floor. There was another knock at the back door. Jane Heslop peeped in.

"Come in, dear. You're not late. Push up you lot," said Miss Proud.

Boys and girls shuffled legs and feet to make space, but their eyes did not move at all.

"Here we go," whispered one of the Hogarths. Other children shifted excitedly.

"Six Five Special," said the television announcer.

A steam train pounded towards them.

"Six Five Special steaming down the line.
Six Five Special right on time.
My heart's a beating 'cause I'll be meeting.
The Six Five Special in the station tonight."
The children joined in
"Elvis is best," said Billy Boustead.
Janice Wright was indignant. "Tommy Steele,"
she hissed.
Miss Proud smiled.
Catherine rolled her eyes.

April 1959 was unusually cold, but the Italian Ryegrass in
the Long Pasture was rippling in the wind. Ben had not
seen such early growth. The sward was even, an unusual
dark green, there were no seed heads and each leaf was
sappy. Sunny Banks had never carried a crop like it.

"It's the artificial," said Bill Henderson. "It's too tall to
put the cows straight in. They'd trample it. We'll let them
out between milkings to strip graze. Ration it by using an
electric fence."

"We should build a new byre, stalls for fifty cows, and
a central feeding passage so we can back a feed trailer
straight in," said Jim.

"Would you have enough grass?" asked Ben.

"Eric Bowman's giving up. We're going to take his
bottom fields."

He was with Edward. They were walking their ponies
through Syke Wood. Its stillness wrapped them. Riding's
rhythms lulled them too.

Edward pointed to a bank of wood anemones. Ben dismounted. His fingers were careful as he picked out the longest stems.

"Grandma will like these," he said.

They stopped regularly to watch or listen. Their ponies snatched at fresh grass. Woodpeckers drummed. A snap of dry twigs signalled roe deer. Rabbits scattered as they moved through a final wicket gate into a field. Huntley Vale spread below them. Curlews bubbled. The boys were happy to listen and stare.

"See the two fields beside the green shed," said Edward. "The Thompsons have taken them off old man Hepple. They're going to buy more cows."

On other evenings they trailed through woods and fields on foot.

"What the hell's that?" said Edward, pointing to movement in a hayfield's lengthening grass.

It was a large animal with a low-slung body. It scuttled erratically.

"Whatever it is, it's feeding," said Ben.

The shape raised its head to either sniff or listen. The black and white stripes were unique.

It was the first live badger they'd seen.

When they moved closer it sank into the grass to hide.

"Just a cub," said Edward when it set off for a hedge.

Ben trapped it with his legs while Edward grabbed a handful of loose skin behind its neck.

Scott was astonished when they carried it back to Whiteside. It was the first he had seen too.

The parish's most enthusiastic amateur photographer was summoned.

"The boys have caught a badger," he was told, disbelievingly, over the phone.

Long John was in the Chapel's pulpit.

"A Schoolmaster always needs help," he told the congregation. "Ben will read the Lessons."

He stood up straight, and read so well, Jack Graham marked him down to take the Sunday School's junior section for bible instruction.

Summer term's exam papers had been marked. Jennifer Quayle once again held top position in the right-hand corner of the back row, but other results had forced radical re-arrangement. Girls had thrived under monthly marks' routine demands because their writing was neat, homework conscientious and most delivered what was demanded on time. Exams were different. Most boys shrugged off pressure created by the ninety-minute deadline, made quicker decisions on the options raised by question selection and could scribble faster. Ben, who had moved up from the half-way mark, took a place in the back row. Almost every girl had been pushed closer to the front.

Mr Smailes, who taught history, was astonished.

It was the first time this predisposition had been demonstrated in a Morwick classroom.

"What is this?" he demanded. "The classroom's back to front."

But Scott was still unhappy with his annual report.

Phrases like "careless", "has problems concentrating", and "talks too much in class" bothered him.

"His heart's not in it," he told Alice.

When he got off the school bus, Totty Farr, primed to mock, was waiting on the village green.

"Grammar School boy," he said.

Ben stopped.

Totty smirked.

"Fancy yer chances?"

Ben tripped him, sat on his chest, and slapped his face.

Totty, shocked that he had been so easily humiliated by a Blazer Boy, slunk off.

It was harvest time at Sunny Banks and he was pleased he was being useful. The tractor he was driving tracked a line of straw bales which Jim threw on the trailer that was being towed behind.

"Whooapp," called Henderson who was stacking.

He pushed down the clutch and put the Ferguson into neutral. The load grew taller so he had to stop and start more often. Jim began to use a pitchfork. Sweating as he skewered each bale before hoisting it.

"Three more," his father said.

Jim wiped his forehead on his forearm and threw up the last bale. Ben pulled on the handbrake and jumped down. The load was roped then Henderson lay on his stomach and extended an arm. Jim cupped his hands, Ben lifted his foot, stepped into them and was thrown up too. Henderson helped him through a final wriggle then they both sat back.

Riding a loaded trailer was like sailing a boat because it swayed over every hump and through every hollow on its way back to the steading. Bill Henderson rested. Ben looked down on unfamiliar hedge tops, over distant fields, or into rushy bottoms. Annie Armstrong's apple crop looked promising, and he wondered, yet again, why Jed Lambert's collie always barked. More work lay ahead. He would pass bales down to his uncle. They would be hoisted onto a clanking elevator while Jim, sweating in the cavity under the shed roof, re-stacked them as tightly as he could.

The boy was hugely content.

CHAPTER FOUR

The strength of a chain

Catherine came to the Grammar School when Ben moved up to Fourth Form. She too was tall and her green eyes were framed by jet black hair.

"You're Ben's sister!" squealed older girls who swarmed round her between lessons. "He's lovely."

She tried to tell him he had admirers but he dismissed it.

His problem was Fifth Form bullies who either spat in his face or kneed him between the legs.

One evening his testicles hurt so much he had to tell Scott.

And in an unusual moment of intimacy his father had examined him.

The right side of his scrotum was badly bruised. A testicle swollen.

"Who did this?"

"Peter Arkless."

"Best keep out of his way."

Scott watched as his eldest son walked to the door.

Farm work was hardening him, he was already strong, clearly pubescent, and would soon be even taller.

It would not be long, he reflected, before bullies like Arkless would have to mend their ways.

Alice eventually won her battle over a television. Scott had grumbled about not wanting square eyed children but was the most regular user after it was installed. He became a news addict and when documentaries on WW2 began to be screened called in his family so they could watch them together. The compounded newsreels were merciless, corpse count off the scale, and the misery of the wounded, or dispossessed, was raw. Alice frowned when footage showing Manningham and other northern cities being bombed was screened. During one raid her sister Doris had missed her tram by seconds. It had taken a direct hit as she watched it pull away.

Scott watched the Dunkirk evacuation with a hard face. He'd fought in the rearguard action and had been among the last to be rescued. Alice sat with him when the North Africa campaign was screened. "Rommel was good," he said. "We were lucky to beat him." Clips covering the German retreat from Moscow were dreadful but those covering the liberation of Concentration Camps were worse. "You have to see it," said Alice when Catherine hid her head in a cushion. "Shows what a good job it was we won."

Ben liked getting the Sunny Banks cows in for evening milking. Most were waiting at Rough Strother's gate. They plodded down the lane as he called the stragglers in.

"Huff-werf, hufff-werff. C'mon. Huff-werf."

Belinda, an especially placid cow, was last to come through.

Her hooves clacked as they crossed the concrete yard and into Jim's new byre.

Most of the forty-eight cows went straight to their stall. He helped to tie them. Just three were uncertain. He encouraged them to take their place while Jim fastened their chains. Milking machines were carried in. Buckets to take milk to the cooler were lined up as well. The feed barrow was pushed through. He and Jim doled out the first cake and started milking. A pulsator clicked rhythmically when he turned on its air.

He went down on one knee, put his head against Tess's flank and unhooked the milking machine's teat cluster. His soothing "steady girl" was muttered through habit. Tess was only interested in eating her cake so attaching the hungry, hissing, teat cups was easy. Her milk frothed through immediately.

"Wish they were all as easy as that," said Jim as they waited for the first cow to finish.

"Not another new blazer," complained Alice. "I can let down your trousers again but can't do anything about this." She swept a palm across his shoulders. He was already much taller than her.

"Arkless keeps hurting me," said Catherine.

She waved a hand over her chest. "He rubs me here."

The outline of her growing breasts was clear.

"Tell him to stop," said Ben.

"I have. It's no good. He runs over every time he sees me. I told him I'd tell you. He just laughed."

Katy Wallace, who sat near the back of his class, had an unusually heavy chest and it had attracted a swarm of gropers.

He'd seen the jostling between lessons and the horrified look on other girls' faces.

Despite her distress, the boys surrounding Katy took turns to plunge a hand inside her bra.

Lawson, a huge youth with livid spots, liked to stand directly behind her and forage two-handed.

He was not going to let that happen to Catherine.

He confronted Arkless in the playground.

His intention to initiate a clash was underlined by language that was formal.

"Lay off my sister."

Arkless's reply was formal too.

"Who's going to stop me?"

Schoolyard scraps tracked near ritual progression. They would begin with an attempt at a headlock, a trip, or a hip throw, then one rival immobilising the other by pinning his arms and sitting on his chest. Punching was a last resort.

So he was shocked when Arkless immediately hit him in the mouth.

He knew his lips had split. Worse still, more humiliation for Catherine loomed, and his pride was threatened too.

His right hand was already hanging low and his left foot was slightly forward. He flung his fist at Arkless's jaw and readied himself for the reaction.

Nothing happened. He'd vanished. Was no longer in front of him. The spot on which he'd been standing was empty. He'd gone.

Ben looked to his left.

Arkless was flat on his back. Eyes gently shut. Unmoving. Knocked out. There was a hole in the sole of his right shoe.

The playground was as stunned as he was.

One reward was immediate elevation to first place on a dining room table.

He did not push for the top position. Other Fourth Form boys automatically gave way.

The canteen was so crowded, teachers trying to grab a meal themselves, had no chance of moderating the anarchy that seethed on the benches behind them.

Third Formers, all of them smaller, many of them timid, were the principal victims because the older boys took most of their food.

Ben's Third Form had been unhappy because the Fourth Former who'd jostled to secure prime place not only heaped his own plate at everyone else's expense but humiliated those trapped in its lower reaches as well.

Egged on by the fawning acolyte who sat beside him he would, when tinned pineapple was the pudding, with taunting deliberation, put just one cube and a single spoonful of custard precisely in the centre of Ben's otherwise empty plate.

His response to canteen tradition was to marshal the boys on his table's lower reaches.

"I'm going to take all I want and these lads–" his gesture covered friends who hoped to prosper under his umbrella– "will too, so there won't be much left when the tray gets down to you. Don't waste time sitting here. Get as many as you can into the queue for seconds. You can have everything you bring to the table."

Dick Wood sat mid-way. He watched Ben take almost a third of the steak and kidney pie and immediately set off with two others. They headed the free-for-all at the second helpings hatch and came back with enough food to heap everyone's plate.

Other tables went short. But boys' dining room rules were simple. Dog would eat dog and the weak, less cunning, or less organised, had to be satisfied with crumbs.

***

It was early on a Saturday morning and Nancy Kerr was shouting at him from the bottom of the stairs.

"Ben Robson, get out of bed and get down here. We're thrashing."

She was in the kitchen talking to Alice when he rushed in.

"We're shorthanded. You know the ropes. Your Mam said you could help."

The stackyard at Earthly Mires was heaving.

A threshing machine held centre position.

The single cylinder Field Marshall that powered the belt which turned its drum chuffed a regular rhythm.

Men waited until he took his place at the grain chutes. His job was to make sure sacks were replaced as soon as they were full.

Children and terriers stood ready to catch rats and mice.

"Let's go," called Alf who was standing, pitchfork ready, on top of the first of a cluster of stacks.

Archie Stoner, the contractor, opened the Field Marshall's throttle, the threshing drum began to whine, and Alf heaved the first sheaf to Geordie Elliott who, sitting on the thresher itself, and unfamiliar in overalls and flat cap, caught it, chopped its string and spilled the stalks onto the spinning blades.

The thumping whoosh, which became continuous as Alf and Geordie settled in, confirmed that grain, straw and chaff were being beaten apart.

Edward's job would be dusty. He was waiting to fork straw into a baler. The Jewson brothers would carry bales to a nearby shed.

Ben checked the first two sacks were firmly hooked, waited for the first grain to spill through, then made sure the stopper which would block the chute when the bag was full, was working.

Empty sacks were heaped to his left. A scale, the correct weights stacked, was on his right.

If he could keep pace he would weigh, then tie, each bag before standing it, ready to be carried up the steps to the granary, against the stackyard wall.

"I can help," said Catherine.

Alice, who was watching with Tom, smiled, waved, and left.

He showed her how to swing the stoppers.

Later he would show her how to make sure the grain in each bag weighed exactly eight stones.

Nancy had cooked a huge dinner. Mashed potato, boiled turnips, and beef mince smothered equally huge plates.

"They were my grandmother's. Kept 'specially to feed hungry men on a day like this," she said as she reached over and ladled out yet more mince for Geordie whose "bless you" was automatic.

Ben and Catherine sat with Edward on a bench that had been brought in so they could join the crowded table.

The men were talking about crop yields, who had died, buyers, who'd got married, and prices.

Edward was more interested in hunting.

"You've got too big for Josh," he said.

"Catherine should be riding him instead."

Work began half an hour after they'd stopped.

Everyone was in rhythm now.

Two men threw up to Geordie when a stack shrank close to ground level.

And both children and terriers chased, and killed, the rodents that swarmed when a stack's last sheaves were being lifted.

A pair of men hoisted sacks of grain onto their backs and slogged across the yard to the granary.

They helped Catherine to weigh out, or Ben at tying, if they fell behind.

"That's the one the cobbler killed his wife with," said Alf as he hoisted the last sheaf.

The stackyard had been emptied.

The Field Marshall's engine was cut.

The last of the straw was forked into the baler.

"You did well," said Alf, as he handed Ben a pound note.

"You too, Catherine. Here's ten shillings."

Her eyes widened. It was much more money than she'd earned before.

And, right on time, Nancy called everyone in for tea.

The mood was celebratory. The stories entertaining.

"I like the Kerrs," said Catherine when she and Ben were being driven home.

He was offered more work as he got older.

He forked manure, rolled or harrowed pasture, thinned turnips, milked many cows, and when summer evenings lengthened helped make hay and harvest corn.

Alice forced him to open a savings account so he hid at least half the notes he earned between the pages of his thickest book.

She insisted he gave up teaching at Sunday School too.

Scott was given a rare hard look.

"I don't want him to be a preacher."

But his father demanded he walked with him each Sunday to the Chapel's morning service where they sat at opposite ends of the rear pew.

The prayers were extempore. So were the vomit splash patterns on his trouser turnups. He enjoyed being noisy

with his friends in Morwick's pubs but his body struggled
to hold endless pints of beer.

"I'm told you've been in the Crown and Mitre," said
Geordie Elliott.

He was leaning against an elevator, Ben was on top of
a half-built stack, and they were waiting for Jack Graham
to bring in another load of straw.

There was no reply.

The Chapel's organist grimaced.

"The strength of a chain is its weakest link."

"I understand that," said Ben.

"Let's hope you do," said Geordie before he
looked away.

CHAPTER FIVE

God knows

Sixth Form was unexpectedly pleasant. Classes were half size, the timetable less frantic, and teachers were relaxed.

"You're almost adult. We'd like to be able to always treat you that way," declared Mr Phipps.

University crooked its finger too.

"If you work hard you could all get a place," promised Miss Moore.

Carol Atkinson's brown eyes became more liquid.

They followed him each time he got on, or off, the school bus.

The games master tried to interest him in First XV rugby. But the team was dominated by boys from Crown Lane who mocked his mistakes.

"It's disappointing you can't stick with it, Robson."

"The buses are at bad times, sir. Takes too long to walk home."

He had taken down his 12 bore. He was going over to Wheelstones and hoped to shoot a rabbit for Meg on the way.

Tom was watching.

"Do you want to come with me?"

Tom nodded.

"You'd better tell Mam first."

Alice pushed him into a jacket.

"I'll pick you up at eight."

"This a shotgun," he said.

"You must walk behind me when it's loaded."

He opened the breech to show Tom it was not.

When they came to Syke Wood's last wicket gate he put a finger to his lips.

"We should see rabbits when we turn that corner."

He loaded two cartridges. Tom was already standing behind him.

"You must be even more careful when I pull back the hammers."

Tom's nod was solemn.

He shot two rabbits and showed him how to gut them.

"What's that?"

"It's the liver."

"Where's his heart?"

"Up in his ribs. Grandma likes me to leave it for her cats. You can see his kidneys here. I left them in too."

Tom examined the emptied abdomen carefully.

Then Ben threaded their hind legs.

"Do you want to carry them?" he asked.

The nod was eager.

"Would you like to fire a shot?"

This time the nod was emphatic.

The third rail on a nearby fence was Tom's height. Ben rested the gun on it and pointed to a thorn bush.

"That's your target."

He showed him how to hold the stock against his right shoulder and use his left hand to steady the barrels.

He pulled the hammer back and used his right hand to support Tom's arm.

"Rest your cheek against the stock, close your left eye, aim along the centre line with your right, and pull the right-hand trigger slowly when you've lined the sight with the middle of the bush."

The bang, and the slash of the shot, satisfied them both.

"Grandma. Look what we've got," said Tom as he burst through her back door.

Josh was moved to Earthly Mires.

It made it easier for Catherine to join the Kerrs out hunting.

"You should have seen her," said Edward.

"She jumped everything."

Duke became even more bad tempered but because he was potent, and his daughters milked well, Henderson kept him on.

The bull pen had been modified so his nose ring was attached to a rope that swung from a head high cable that had been strung diagonally between the feed manger and his drinking bowl.

"You can open the door to fork in his hay but don't step inside the cable line because he'll have you," warned Jim.

The bull shook his head when he saw them. He lowered it threateningly. A front foot slowly scraped the floor.

Strings of saliva hung from his nose and dribbled off his jaw.

The rope knotted to the brass ring that had been looped through his nostrils was permanently soaked.

The TV in the living room confirmed the next programme would be 'Top of the Pops'.

Catherine squeaked and wriggled deeper into the sofa.

Mop headed groups of four pounded out selections from that week's Top Twenty.

When Scott opened a door to see why there was so much noise she was hugging a cushion.

"Have you no homework?"

"Sshh, Dad. Sshh. I'll do it later."

The likes and dislikes of Gerry from the Pacemakers were being listed on screen.

"Gerry likes Jam Tarts, Baked Beans, Seaside Holidays and Cornish Pasties," a confident voice declared.

Still photos confirmed these pronouncements.

Scott watched with disbelief.

"Good grief," he grunted after being told Gerry disliked tripe.

He shook his head and retreated.

Ben knew almost all the Chapel's lay preachers, liked most of them, but found their unquestioning belief in the omnipotence of an all-seeing deity joltingly naive.

Sermons were crammed with rural metaphors and almost always drawn from personal experience.

Bill Richardson was in the pulpit. He farmed Lockey Tops and milked a typical herd of cows.

His style when helping his congregation re-confirm its dedication to a virtuous lifestyle was always anecdotal.

"I was in the yard helping the driver unload his feed lorry."

"I asked him if he thought it would rain?"

"His answer was 'God knows.'"

"Friends. That's exactly how he said it."

"Just like that."

"God knows."

Richardson shook his head to underline the flippancy of Wagon Driver's observation.

He repeated its offhand tone.

"God knows."

Richardson leaned forward. His posture and tone became confidential.

"But let me tell you, Friends."

"God does know."

"God knows everything."

Geordie Elliott lifted his head.

"Hallelujah."

He was echoed by several fervent "Amens".

Ben was pleased his father had promised that when he was eighteen he would not have to go to Chapel again.

It was mid-afternoon and Josh was still enjoying himself.

The field was down to half a dozen. Those that could not keep pace had either pulled up or were trailing well to the rear.

Catherine rode directly behind the Field Master and Alf Kerr.

The hounds were stretched in a long line and the fox still ran strongly.

They caught a glimpse of the Huntsman on the far side of a steep valley.

"This bit can be tricky," warned Field Master as they headed downhill towards a succession of fences and stone walls.

Alf glanced back at Catherine who crooked two fingers over her martingale strap and laughed.

They took the lot, a couple of them with heart stopping drops, then splashed through a stream.

There was yet another jump and a long canter across a broad field.

Alf opened a wicket and they trotted into some whins where they were surrounded by a mill of restlessly sniffing hounds.

Someone said, "gone to ground", reins were released, and horses stood, heads down, recovering their breath.

"You were good," said Alf. "Josh was too."

"He's perfect," said Catherine, burying her face in his mane.

Josh, now cropping hungrily at yellow grass, was not distracted.

"We're going to leave Charlie where he is," said Field Master.

He turned to Catherine. "You should not be here."

She thought she was being told off then noticed his smile.

"Ever thought about Pony Club?"

They found the nearest road and trotted back to their wagons and trailers.

It was typical of Morwick's regular Sixth Form parties.

Someone's parents were away for the weekend and their home had been invaded.

Carol Atkinson pushed Ben into a corner, wrapped her arms around him and rested her head on his chest.

"Got you."

She stood back, held his face in her hands, and kissed him.

He was too full of beer to resist. They explored each other's tongues.

"Let's go outside," she whispered.

They found a bench in the back garden.

Her body was extraordinarily relaxed.

"How far do you want to go?"

Carol's question could have been a joke.

Grammar School boys coded sexual progress numerically when they were boasting among themselves.

Number One was holding hands.

Number Five was the removal of a bra.

Number Ten was the whole way – an ambitious feat that few considered because the many threats raised by pregnancy were real.

Carol's hands had already done something which was not on a list that highlighted only what a boy might get away with.

Girls were assumed to be passive.

"As far as you want," Ben replied.

She hauled him to his feet. "Let's find somewhere warmer."

It was a fine spring morning and the yards at Sunny Banks were busy.

Fieldwork beckoned but the morning routine had still to be completed.

Henderson was buzzing about on his new Dexta shifting bedding with a front-end loader.

Ben was sweeping up loose straw.

Jim was forking in Duke's hay.

The door to the bullpen was open.

Duke's shoulders suddenly filled the gap.

His knees were on Jim's chest and he was raking it with alternate horns. A sequence of wet snaps confirmed Jim's ribs had cracked.

His hands beat uselessly at the massive head and neck.

Ben took to Duke with his brush. Forcing bristles into his left eye.

The bull ignored him.

He grabbed the pitchfork and jabbed at Duke's muzzle.

There was blood but no other response.

He attacked the eye with a single tine and angled the shaft so he could drive it deeper.

Perhaps reach the brain!

Henderson chugged into the yard with more straw.

His reaction was immediate.

"Out the way," he shouted as he lined the tractor up.

Then, "keep your head down," as he rammed the loader home.

The bull, almost a ton of bone and muscle, was forced back.

An ambulance was called.

A fragment of torn rope dangled from Duke's blood covered nose ring. His left eye hung from a tendril of tissue like an overripe plum.

A new canteen opened its doors at the beginning of the summer term.

The dining room's tables stood well apart, there were chairs instead of benches, and food was served over a long stainless steel counter instead of through a narrow hatch.

"Boys and girls will eat together," said the Deputy Head.

Ben took top dog position.

When Fifth Form lackeys came back with food he grabbed the trays.

The girls who were sitting with them stared at him blankly.

"Are you serving?" asked Judy Clark.

He hesitated. Taking food off a younger boy was one thing. Taking it off a girl was another.

Judy was decisive.

"Give them to me. I can do it quicker than you."

He surrendered.

Fifth Form boys were goggle eyed.

When he went for seconds he was given a huge plateful by the dinner ladies.

When pudding came Judy served that too.

Everyone ate well.

Conversation across the table was friendly.

Lunchtime's conversion from anarchy to order, made possible by the restraining presence of Judy and other girls, had been secured within the snap of a finger.

He walked over to see his grandparents that weekend.

Middle Paisley was a monochrome sweep of unusually lush rye grass. There was no longer a carpet of flowers.

He had to detour around the dyke backs to avoid trampling the crop.

A hedge between Bolisher and Woodside had been taken out as well.

"We've got to make more silage," explained Jim. "Hay's too catchy."

Kit sat in his fireside chair.

Meg put out cakes, buns and tea.

"Your grumpy Grandad doesn't like these new machines," she said.

"Not happy with that stuff that comes in blue bags either," said Kit.

"Nitram?" said Ben.

"That's the one," said Kit. "It'll suck the life out of the soil."

A new delivery was in the yard.

He flicked a label on one of the sacks.

Its nitrogen content was 34.5 per cent.

"How much are you putting on?" he asked Jim.

"As much as we can. It's magic. We want to take at least two cuts. More yield off the same acres."

Judy Clark stopped him in a school corridor.

"Why don't you have a steady girlfriend?"

"Don't like the pictures," said Ben who found the fumbling rituals that rustled the length of the Majestic's double-seated back row repugnant.

Judy was standing eye to eye. Her posture inquisitorial.

The previous weekend he had seen her in the front seat of a sports car driven by a university student who lived on Crown Lane.

"We could go somewhere else," she prompted.

He still hesitated.

"Come on, Ben Robson. What more does a lady have to do?"

He wanted to tell her that he loathed school courtship routines. Did not want anyone else to know where, or where not, his interest or affection might lie.

But he ducked out.

"Not be so bossy," he said.

And walked away.

Their headmaster, nicknamed 'Tomato' because his face was florid, kept a Scottish tawse in the bottom left hand drawer of his desk.

Ben knew this because there had been at least six occasions when he'd watched it being taken out before being told to bend over.

It was a malevolent leather tool. Perhaps two feet long that had been slit at the whip end to make a wicked vee.

Its damage was distinctive.

Each stinging stroke – there had never been less than three – had left a characteristic, double-stamped bruise just below the joint on his right hip.

On the last occasion, just over a year ago, it had drawn blood.

This was why, on the second last day of his final term, he had skipped morning assembly, taken a deep breath, crept into the head's study, lifted the tawse from its drawer, and taken it home.

That evening he carved his name on the napped underside and underscored the gouges with ink.

He returned it the following morning after taking an even bigger breath before opening the study door again.

His "A" level results were modest. But so were almost everyone else's.

Redbrick University in Manningham had offered him a place on its English course. He had been told to turn up at the beginning of October.

The County's Education Committee would pay his fees and cough up an annual £340 grant.

He set out to tell Meg and Kit.

His pace was slow and his mood detached.

An avenue of beech trees ran through Syke Wood.

Its vault of interlaced branches was majestic.

Their leaves were beginning to turn. It would not be long before they glowed like stained glass windows.

He had a sense the world was wide.

He thought he could survive within it.

He was aware he was being tugged towards a future that Meg and Kit, perhaps even Scott and Alice, could not imagine.

But he did want to be unfettered.

Live on his own terms.

He also knew that if he did break rules he must not get caught.

After he left the wood he leaned on a wicket gate.

Wheelstones lay ahead and smoke was lifting from the farmhouse chimney.

Red machines and a blue tractor stood in what had been the stackyard.

A double-spanned shed with a blindingly white roof dominated what was already being called the back steading.

The byres that surrounded the cobbled yard had been abandoned.

More stock than the farm had ever carried was grazing Bolisher and Woodside.

He wondered, not for the first time, how his grandparents had earned enough to raise a family.

They were thrifty but had never been poor.

Had always been respected when they attended Chapel.

When his grant cheque arrived, he banked it.

CHAPTER SIX

Discipulum

Seminar Room 12 at Redbrick hid at the end of a long corridor on the twelfth floor of a steel and glass block which leaned against a refined main building that struggled to suppress a cultured shudder.

A Students Union, framed by a car park, sports fields, and attractive clusters of trees, sprawled beneath.

Manningham, long terrace rows, high-rise flats, teeming carriageways, hefty office blocks, smoking factories, sport stadia, church steeples and polished railway lines, thrummed beyond.

Ben was wearing a jacket and tie. Most of the other males lined up in front of their Course Tutor for the first time had favoured conformity too.

Almost half those present were ladies, or was it girls? Some had put on makeup. All wore nylons. Margaret – "I prefer Maggie" – had dressed in a surprisingly tight skirt.

Everyone was aware that over the next three years they would be bound, almost umbilically, by shared coursework. But some had still to pluck up courage to look around.

Balfour, who was older, and had already claimed he'd written a book, tried to dominate. His voice was cultured and lazy. Others who had come in from public school confirmed similar confidence and poise.

Students from state schools revealed a range of regional accents. A frowning West African – it was being whispered he was a prince – dominated the front row.

A Moroccan and an Aussie peppered the assembly too.

"You are visible proof of the educational renaissance that is sweeping the UK. There are more students registered at Redbrick than there have ever been and, speaking frankly, the faculty is struggling to accommodate you all," Course Tutor told the room.

"There may be some short-term timetable hitches, but we expect that within a fortnight these wrinkles will have been ironed out. You can contribute to the smooth running of the Department by being punctual when attending lectures or tutorials and presenting your coursework on time."

"The University stages regular lunchtime addresses. I recommend you take advantage of them. Last year it hosted a range of internationally recognised academics. Politicians and other national figures of interest are also invited."

"The Students Union supports clubs and societies that offer valuable service as well. However, it is at the same time home to distractions that do not always sit well with disciplined academic study and I counsel you to be cautious in your approach."

"The campus doctor holds regular surgeries. You should register with him. A receptionist arranges appointments. I hope few of you will require his attention."

Course Tutor paused before shattering expectations nursed by teenagers who had left home for the first time.

"You will of course be aware of the concept in loco parentis?"

"It means that unless you are adults, have achieved your majority at twenty-one, the University is legally obliged to accept responsibility on behalf of your parents for your safety, welfare and wellbeing."

"It will not shirk its duty of care. There may indeed be occasions when it will be compelled to undertake defined parental function."

He paused. His practised eye rested on each of the group in turn.

"I hope that as far as the individuals in this room are concerned the University is never obliged to assume these duties. In loco parentis does not apply to everyone present. Mr Imano, Mr Balfour, Mr Farid and Miss Gilchrist are of course exempt. If any of those still legally a minor require further explanation, or have relevant questions, I'm always available for advice."

Balfour smirked. Course Tutor's message was clear. If females in the group were younger than twenty-one they were just girls after all. And Ben, along with other males, was technically still a boy.

Assumptions on adulthood and independence which may have flowered when anxious parents waved goodbye were already being adjusted.

He caught a 47 bus. It joined a long queue at a red light. It was his first traffic jam. He wondered why he was not excited.

His digs, a fading five-bedroom house which stood behind a ragged privet hedge and scruffy flower bed, were in Poplar Avenue.

His landlady, a weary widow, struggled with not just her own children but two other students each paying her a vital £4.10s a week.

The University's Great Hall was jammed.

Student societies were tracking down new members and freshers were their prey.

Film Soc attracted him.

Drama Club, which was being drummed by an over-excited, pop-eyed man with a straggly beard, could take a running jump.

The University newspaper was Discipulum.

The drinking club styled itself Gurgle.

A third-year student wearing a short back and sides haircut, frayed sports jacket, dirty white collar, stained tie, baggy flannels and scruffy brogues tapped the top of his head with a rolled newspaper.

"You've got to be a rugby player."

Ben shook his head.

"Basketball? Water Polo?"

He shook his head again.

A card school dominated a corner of the Common Room.

The circle of heads was deep into the skein of bluff and counter bluff that threaded Three Card Brag.

The pot was kicked off when each player threw in a penny piece. Opening bets were almost always a penny too. Those playing blind, without looking at their cards, obliged everyone else to put in double. Most coins in the mounds that accumulated before the last-but-one hand was either folded, or seen, were copper. When the circle shrank to just two or three players, the most confident sometimes raised bets to six pence but plays which demanded more than a shilling were rare.

Scott, who claimed he had been able to send Alice all his army pay because he won so regularly, had taught his children to brag while making bets with dried peas and butter beans instead of coins.

He had frowned on reckless play, concentrating instead on encouraging them to adopt a calculating style that reflected genuine odds.

Ben had watched long enough to see that the players in front of him were careless. And the regular winners, those sitting behind the biggest piles of money, dominated only because everyone else was afraid of losing – were being bluffed out.

"Room for another?" he asked.

The circle shuffled to make space.

"Fresher, eh?" observed the dealer as he flicked him his first card.

Sometimes he threw in immediately, won two virtually uncontested pots with hands as modest as a low pair, then he took something like four shillings with an almost unchallenged flush.

No one seemed to notice.

An hour later he picked up a running flush. The six, seven, and eight of clubs. It was a hand to pray for unless – unless – someone was holding a higher sequence or, heaven forbid, three cards with the same number – an extraordinarily elusive prile.

He doubled his stake, the maximum allowed, as often as he could.

Once again no one appeared to notice.

But when bets had lifted to a florin a pitch just two other players were left.

Spectators began to gather.

He knew he must be gambling against hands almost as strong as his or perhaps even better.

Scott's harshest criticism came, not when a good hand had lost, but when the best hand had been thrown in early.

"How can you possibly win if you fling the top cards away?"

Running flushes were rare.

He'd stick this one out. Either pay double to see what the other survivor was holding, or be seen himself, the moment just two players were left.

Bets moved up to half-a-crown. Then five shillings. There was a stir when Ben put down a ten-shilling note.

The other players followed.

He raised the bets to a pound.

It was crunch time.

"I'm raising you two pounds," said the one with a Brummie accent.

"Fuck it," said the Welshman. "I've run out of cash."

He scribbled a cheque and threw it on the table.

The Brummie put in two pounds again.

Ben raised his bet to four pounds.

"I'm out," said Welshman throwing down a king, queen, jack.

Brummie wrote a cheque for eight pounds.

"See you."

He put down his running flush.

Someone said "Jesus".

Brummie's cards slammed down.

Necks craned.

Ace, king, queen.

Not quite enough.

"I had to stay with him," he pleaded, looking round the table for support.

Ben scooped his winnings and sat back in his chair.

He put the notes and cheques in his wallet.

He picked the silver out of the pile too.

"Who's got a bag?" he said, pointing to the copper coins and three penny pieces. "Let's go to the bar."

"How big was the pot?" someone dared to ask.

"Twenty-four pounds," he replied.

The beer that was bought later cost less than two shillings a pint.

Rounds were shared after the bag of pennies had been emptied.

"Let's go for a Chinese," said Brummie.

The menu was exotic. Ben was encouraged to try Peking Duck.

"We'll go for a curry next time," promised Malcom "Fuck It" Price.

News that a Common Room card game had been settled with cheques spread fast.

Even Miss Gilchrist was keen to discover if the rumour was true.

Course Tutor stopped him in the corridor.

"Was it really twenty-four pounds?" he asked.

When Ben confirmed this he was given a curious look.

He went back to Whiteside for Christmas.

Alice kissed him and Scott pretended not to notice his much longer hair.

Tom wanted to see his books.

He pulled out "Brave New World", "A Farewell to Arms" and "1984".

"Alf Kerr's riddling potatoes tomorrow," said Catherine.

He decided to go to Wheelstones the day after instead.

"We need eighty bags," said Alf. "Shops have gone crazy."

Ben forked potatoes out of the clamp onto the riddle's ramp.

Soil and pig potatoes, those too small to sell, were shaken through its vibrating mesh.

Nancy stood on one side of the tray picking out stones and green or damaged potatoes too big to be sieved out.

Catherine, eyes sharp, hands snatching, policed the other.

Alf bagged the shop quality potatoes that dropped off the end and swung them onto a scale.

Edward made sure each sack weighed four stones, tied its neck with wire and put it in the wagon.

They stopped at the halfway mark to grab a re-heated dinner.

The palm of his left hand had blistered.

"You know Jim's getting married?" said Meg. "One of the Waltons. Good family. Pleasant girl."

Kit shifted in his chair.

"They're moving in. We're taking the cottage behind Tot Swinburne's place."

Ben looked round their kitchen.

The range, its cast iron carefully blacked and stainless-steel handles gleaming, dominated the back wall.

A soot-stained kettle rested by the hob.

Oil cloth protected the table.

Rag carpets covered the stone floor.

A pantry hid behind a door that even now was rarely open.

It was where Meg had put milk in flat pans to settle before being skimmed. Her butter had been stored there too. The marble bench that held centre position was surrounded by stone shelves.

Meat hooks stabbed its ceiling.

Its single window faced north.

It had been his grandparents' refrigerator.

He had rarely been inside.

The only time Meg had spanked him was when he'd sneaked in and left the door open.

Jim would rip everything out.

"Pat Walton?"

Jim laughed.

"Sometime in August."

Gladys passed Ben more bread.

"We've moved onto AI," said Henderson. "Inseminating the best cows with semen taken from bulls with high performing daughters and using Angus on the rest."

Meticulous national yield recording had underlined that Britain's top cows milked like machines.

When he was a boy a veteran that had topped 2,000 gallons over a single lactation had been famous.

Now Jim could look forward to managing at least half a dozen that could beat that.

The Angus crosses would be sold for beef.

Quick turnover for useful money instead of persisting with a low-grade milker that only grudgingly earned more than she cost.

"Herd bulls have been made redundant," said Jim.

"Good job too," said Gladys.

"A better milk price would make life easier," said Henderson. "Sometimes think we're running faster just to stand still."

"You look better with longer hair," said Judy Clark.

He was sitting with her in the back room of The Comet.

The length of her thigh was pressed against him.

He would remember its softness for days.

They stayed with the noisy students they were drinking with when they moved on to Morwick's new nightclub later.

When he was not slogging, head down, in the library, he liked to rest in the Common Room.

People watching was an underrated pastime, he thought.

An underweight, dark-haired youth, with huge spectacles and an unnaturally pale face was once again lolling loosely in his seat.

His eyes commanded attention. The whites had a pink tinge, his pupils were as big as buttons and his stare was vacant.

"Who is he?" he asked Brummie.

"Jez. A nutter from London. Always gulping down some sort of pill."

Brummie's nose had wrinkled.

"Are you going to play cards?"

Ben shook his head.

He treated three card brag like work.

Beer was expensive. He played to pay for it.

Always did his best to harvest a big win from a pair of smart arses who appeared at lunchtime each Wednesday and opened their betting with two shilling pieces.

And had twice been forced to endure a tense shift early on a Friday evening so he could stick to his weekly budget and not have a dry weekend.

His grant cheque was still untouched. His meticulous approach to money was Methodist.

He was nursing a pint at the Student Union bar when Farid walked in.

"Come with me," he demanded, swivelled on his heels, and walked out.

Ben had to follow him through a maze of corridors before he could catch his eye.

"I want to show you something."

They came to a door.

"Discipulum" it read.

Farid's eyes were hard.

"You are going to take this seriously."

A large room was stuffed with people and four clusters of desks.

He recognised Daryl the Aussie, who made a joke about joining the Disciples, and Maggie, who ignored him.

A tilted bench, smothered in page layout sheets and cuttings, stretched the length of the furthest wall.

A long notice board, thick with page plans and scribbled messages, had been screwed in above it.

A calendar topped by a pin-up with a deep cleavage and wide smile, a sheaf of horse racing pages, theatre schedules, cinema postings and a hook on which the most recent issues of "Discipulum" swung, dominated another.

"This one's the least interesting," said Chris who had been introduced as editor.

It paraded a list of Students Union office holders and members of the committees they chaired.

Farid tugged his arm again.

"Ever been in a dark room?"

He led him through more corridors, put his ear against a door, knocked, got an OK and pulled him quickly in.

The room was in shadow. An enlarger, cameras, trays, a sink, and a stooping figure glowed red.

Photographer Phil shook his hand and took him through the development process.

"This is the most interesting bit," he said, selecting a contact sheet. "We've space for just one picture. So which is the best shot?"

There were fifteen miniatures of a Cabinet Minister who had delivered the lunchtime lecture.

He had a face, wore a suit, looked like a goldfish in some frames and passably human in others.

"We play these straight," said Phil. "The raised fist when his head's tilted backwards is the most dramatic."

He slotted the negative into the enlarger and switched it on.

Shadows, like trout in Stotts Becks, began to shift on the printing paper.

When Cabinet Minister began to surface, Phil used his hands to block selected areas from light.

This softened the background and underlined his fist.

Satisfied with the result he slipped the print into fixer then hung it up to dry.

"Chris might want to crop it. Well judged trim can make a lot of difference."

"Got a camera?" asked Farid.

He shook his head.

"I've a spare. It's 35mm so it's not a Brownie. I'll show you how to set the shutter speed, adjust the aperture, and fine-tune focus tomorrow."

"Then we'll go to the Lyceum. Get some pictures of John Stotch."

He was surprised at the liberties Farid was able to take.

He had watched Stotch being interviewed.

But the actor, who had been accommodating while being quizzed, became wary when Farid stalked forward.

"Oh, go on then," he said resignedly, smoothing his hair when the camera was pushed in his face.

Ben was busting to get a shot of his prominent teeth.

He caught Farid's eye, got the go-ahead, knelt at Stotch's feet, and waited until he had thrown his head back to laugh.

"Fine set of piano keys," Farid said later. "You lost your focus. Otherwise not bad."

"We're going to post a pin-up every issue," Chris told his Disciples.

Maggie chuckled. It would not take long to list the vain and target the willing.

The first poses were demure. A friendly smile beneath a neat hairstyle with perhaps an inch, just a touch, of leg above skirt height thrown in.

"You'd be amazed," said Farid. "Some invite me to their flats. When they see my camera I have to calm them down."

Maggie gave him the name of a girl he'd seen in the library.

Auburn hair, attractive freckles and rumoured to have a long-term boyfriend contracted overseas.

When her picture was published, she was wearing a man's shirt.

Nothing else.

His picture had been taken side-on. The length of her naked right leg, exposed almost to waist height, had tripped a shockwave.

Nor was it possible to misread the come-hither tilt to her chin.

"How did you manage that?" he was asked. "It wasn't your shirt, was it?"

It was her boyfriend's.

She'd taken her bra off as well.

But because his shirt was heavy it had not been obvious.

"Fancy a trip with Daryl to London?" said Chris.

"Universal Herald is the latest underground newspaper. It's run by hippies who stick pins in everyone they can."

"They'll give us an interview. They liked our bum quiz. Thought it was suitably anarchic."

It had been Ben's idea. Present a page of bare bums, and list of names, in quiz form with a prize for identifying what belonged to who.

One had been his own. Maggie and a couple of other girls had been contributors.

Alice had muttered "after all these years" when she'd picked out the right one that Easter.

"They're running an LSD fest on Saturday. A psychedelic love in. Got to be lots of drugs. Probably policemen as well. They'll give us an interview first."

The UH front men were full of themselves.

Egos almost as big as their hair.

"We do this. We do that. Aren't we clever?"

They were certainly different and had moved on from sticking pins.

Their attack on middle class comfort, suburban ideals, and an establishment which encouraged complacency was full on.

"If it's standing up, we want to knock it down," the boss man said.

Their weapons included nakedness, the pleasures of indiscriminate love, subterranean publicity channels and unrelenting advocacy of the many benefits of being stoned.

The Love Fest was disappointing.

The auditorium was only half full.

Posturing had nevertheless been endless.

One narcissist posed languidly in the same corner all night.

"Isn't he cool?" said a passerby.

"He's a prick," said Daryl.

Even so Ben snapped him.

Others leaped round dramatically.

"Look at us. We're cool too."

One group pushed half a dozen imitation classical statues into line.

Plastic beer glasses were wedged, penis-style, between each crotch and bum.

"Sodomy is fun," they chanted desperately.

Bored with that they began to build a beer glass snake.

May's light and warmth unsettled him.

New leaves were whispering.

Birds were busy.

He could smell fresh grass.

The cows would be out.

He writhed in his seat in Seminar Room 12.

He threw desperate glances at the open sky behind him and the trees and space below.

Course Tutor was fascinated.

How much prompting, he asked himself, would it take to persuade young Robson to shin down a drainpipe to escape?

A foursome was on stage and its music was heavy.

The lights that probed the Redbrick Union's recreation hall flicked silhouettes of tossing heads and thrashing legs against its ceiling and walls.

Colours shifted, bass chords became even more insistent, and Ben was dancing alone.

He allowed himself to be taken wherever the music led.

A circle began to form around him.

Rhythmic clapping began.

He was transported.

Hazel, who had branded him unremittingly straight, was puzzled.

Her frown deepened as he danced on and on.

She was watching someone reaching within the music for something impossible to find.

"He's like a mountain moving," whispered the thin Hindu who was standing beside her.

"Mountain perhaps," thought Hazel. "But sad, so intriguingly sad, as well."

CHAPTER SEVEN

Counterculture

He'd spent the summer in isolation.
Moving through a tunnel of work.

Putting up fences, beating grouse, stacking bales, milking his uncle's cows, repairing drystone walls, and banking money.

So he had still to discover the culture bomb he'd heard hissing earlier that year had exploded.

The first issue of Discipulum had already been printed.

Chris had been to Haight Ashbury.

His frontpage headline was "Tune in. Drop out. Rebel".

More boys were wearing longer hair and brighter clothes.

More girls were on the pill.

Mini-skirts were even shorter.

Spliffs prospered.

Jeans flared.

And so did protest.

Britain's youth sensed unimagined freedoms and was desperate to stick its fingers up the establishment's nose.

"We're going to be busy," said Farid.

He was snapping students moving across a quadrangle.

Standard male dress was collar length hair, a pullover and jeans.

Some were wearing kaftans and permed afros.

"Something's happening. They're calling it counterculture. Want to challenge everything. There's subversion. Can't you smell it?"

"Come on," said Hazel.

She was tiny. Slim waist, beguiling legs, and curly hair.

"Let me take you to the cinema."

She knew he was working on Thomas Hardy for his thesis and "Far from the Madding Crowd" was showing in town.

He sat with her in the stalls and stirred uneasily when Gabriel discovered Bathsheba's flock was in the wrong field.

"Could you do that?" she whispered after Oak had stabbed a sheep in the lower gut to let gas that was killing it escape.

"If I had to."

She stiffened in shock.

Rod Crowe was the Students Union president.

Its Council Chamber was packed.

Standing room only unless there was space to sit on a step or room to squat on the floor.

He was demanding seats for undergraduate representatives on the University's Senate and Management Board.

In loco-parentis was being challenged.

"We must have a voice," he insisted. "Our opinions must be heard."

No one disagreed.

An open meeting with the University Vice-Chancellor was to be staged in the Great Hall immediately afterwards.

Crowe would demand "No education without representation".

"If Sir Stanley rejects this we walk out."

Ben, camera in hand, stood behind a curtain.

Sir Stanley stood on stage alone.

The Great Hall was jammed.

Not all the students were agitators. Some had come to watch.

Crowe, a placard in each hand, repeated his petition.

Sir Stanley dismissed it.

Crowe raised his arms.

"Everybody out."

Everyone left.

Sir Stanley gauged the exit.

Science undergraduates and postgraduates had shown him their backs as well.

He heard the shutter of Ben's camera trip.

His face was grave.

"I can see I have made a mistake."

But the University Council rejected Crowe's demands outright.

When it met again a month later, students sat outside the chamber, choked the corridor, and would not let the delegates leave.

Journalists and photographers from both national and regional press were covering the blockade.

They were joined by TV when it became a siege.

Chris, Farid and Ben waited with them in the University's entrance lobby.

"Stalemate," said a weary reporter from the Manningham Telegraph.

"Hope we're not here all night," said a BBC cameraman as he lit yet another cigarette.

Somewhere around ten o'clock there was a stir.

"They're coming out."

The men, all middle aged, wearing trilby hats and overcoats, and carrying briefcases, were being given a hard time. Floor space was scarce and many stumbled.

"Lie down," yelled Crowe.

Their exit would be without dignity. They could only move forward if they trod on arms or legs.

Girls yelped with pain.

Boys resisted.

Tempers flared.

"Bloody brilliant," said BBC, hoisting his camera.

His sound man leaned into the corridor by hanging over a double door.

Some Councillors fought back. Hats were lost, spectacles slipped, and many men were tripped.

Flash bulbs popped. Then popped again.

Janitors and secretaries watched open mouthed.

"You should be ashamed of yourselves," one shouted.

Sir Stanley, grimly clutching his briefcase and hat, was first to struggle through.

He smoothed his hair, straightened his coat and faced a battery of notebooks, questions and cameras.

"This is a sad day," he said. "They have asked to be taken seriously, be accepted as adults, yet this is what they do."

Newspaper and news bulletin editors agreed.

Discipulum's reports covered several pages.

Chris annoyed almost everyone by tacking "No" to the left of the paper's masthead.

Even so a thousand extra copies of "No Discipulum" were sold.

Some student journalists raged at the bruises on some girl's arms and legs.

There were allegations some Councillors had deliberately grabbed at hair.

But the editorial was contrary.

"What else do you expect if you descend to the level of dirty corridor planking?"

He was at a party when Hazel hunted him down.

She knew he had a bedsit.

"It always comes to this," she whispered as she stroked his cheek.

"Your place or mine?"

Chris was excited.

He had been told the anti-Vietnam war demonstration outside the American Embassy in London would be huge.

"We need to get there before the demonstrators."

He was emphatic.

Policemen were already taking position in the gardens and on the grassed area that fronted the building.

Play would begin later. They were marking the pitch.

Ben looked for somewhere detached. He wanted elevation, to be inconspicuous, and have near instant access to flare ups between police and students as well.

It was not going to be easy. The area in front of the Embassy offered the only high ground, but it was a fortress, and he was not going to climb a tree.

He frowned.

Tension was mounting.

It would not be long before he, and others like him, would be pushed back.

A well-dressed woman stood directly in front of him.

"Discipulum?"

He nodded.

"I'm familiar with it."

Her accent was American.

"Since its coverage of the Redbrick sit-in and visit to Universal Herald."

She measured him with level eyes.

"Want to come inside?"

Her head had flicked towards the Embassy.

There was only one answer.

She studied him even more carefully.

"Give me your camera."

She lifted an eyebrow.

"Don't worry. You'll get it back."

"Walk directly behind me and don't look round."

He followed her towards a columned portico. Her overcoat was brown.

She showed a pass to a senior policeman. Then moved towards the Embassy's steps.

She showed her pass again.

This time it was US soldiers who stepped aside.

Sentries stood at the double front door.

They saluted.

She swung left and stood at a hatch. Someone behind its glass pushed out a form.

"He needs your name, address, and signature."

She counter signed then slid it back.

She led him up wide, shallow stairs into a reception area and pointed to a cushioned bench.

"I'll be back in fifteen minutes."

He watched her walk to one of many doors, produce her pass, and be let through.

A line of veranda-like rails had been positioned immediately above the entrance lobby.

He stood against them and looked out.

More police had arrived.

Two men wearing casual clothes, each carrying a long lensed camera, were leaving the building.

Chris and Farid would be wondering where he was.

Browncoat was carrying two files when she returned.

They sat down.

"You can call me Mary. It's not my real name but it will do."

"What do you know about the counterculture movement?"

She interpreted his stare as "not a lot".

"I'm going to show you some photographs. Tell me if you recognize anybody."

The first, A4 size and good quality, was Joe Cohen.

Ben shook his head.

Mick Barker's picture came up later.

He shook his head again.

She sat back.

"Have you seen any Frenchmen?"

"Anyone from Germany?"

"The States?"

She lifted her second file.

"Have you seen him?"

It was Terence. A man he did not like. He was older than most Redbrick students. Unusually well-scrubbed and confident, he often sat with House Committee office holders, enjoying obvious camaraderie but sharing none of their work.

He'd seen him kissing Peggy Butler one lunchtime. Like a predator. Mouth wide open, face and lips red. Licking at her like she was free ice cream.

Browncoat was pleased.

"Do you see him every day?"

"At least once a fortnight."

"When was the last time?"

"Earlier this week."

"Terence is a paid agitator. We think we know who funds him."

She showed him many other faces.

Mainly men, late twenties, and none looking at the camera.

He recognised just one. A slim man whom he'd mistakenly slotted as a mature student. Perhaps thirty years old.

"He didn't know this was being taken."

Her eyes crinkled.

"He did not pose. Would not have done either. Nor will he be surprised we have his picture on file."

A stone hit a window.

The gardens and lawn were being wrecked.

Police and demonstrators wrestled with each other across heaving lines.

"Can I have my camera?"

She smiled.

"If you wait I'll give you something a great deal better."

A volley of missiles hit the building.

Some windows were smashed. A half-brick skidded across the reception floor and hit a wall.

Skittering, side-stepping, police horses were being ridden in.

Another window shattered.

She tapped his arm.

"I think we should move back."

"Vietnam is a mess," she said when they sat down. "But demonstrations like this are being organised to de-stabilise western government. Not to protest against the war itself. More unrest, and some serious violence is expected in Germany, France and," she waved a hand towards the windows, "perhaps the UK.

"Later this year. Maybe next?

"The anarchy, drugs like marijuana, and free love promoted by so-called hippie leaders, through underground newspapers like Universal Herald, are examples of the many lures being used by controllers to bring noisy young people, like those out there, on side. Be their obedient army, create confusion and add weight to their demands."

He wanted to ask who the boss was, and why they would do this, but she was already standing up.

"I'll be twenty to thirty minutes. Don't leave. You won't regret the wait."

There were ten prints, still dark room fresh, in the package she gave him.

"They're for Terence," she said.

Policemen's limbs were flailing, some students were shouting, others screaming, and horses were being used as weapons.

"It's up to you how you use them. It would not be wise to credit them to us and if you did we would of course deny it."

"This briefing will be useful to your editor," she said handing over a sealed envelope.

"Do not show it to anyone else. If he's a genuine journalist he will protect his source. You should tell him that."

Ben pushed it into his shirt pocket.

She handed over his camera and held out her hand.

He shook it.

She left.

"Where the hell have you been?" said Chris.

Farid glowered.

He showed the photos.

"Fuck me," said Chris.

Farid shuffled through them.

"I haven't got anything better than this."

"How did you get them?"

"Tell you later."

They began work that night.

Farid put up a static camera and photographed each print.

"We can crop and re-print as much as we like now," he said.

He circled an index finger and thumb around a girl cowering under a police baton.

"They are good."

Chris read Browncoat's briefing, watched the news in the Common Room, returned to his desk and switched on a radio.

He was still there when Farid and Ben came in with an armful of prints.

"If we handle this properly we'll have better coverage than some nationals."

When Discipulum was printed it hit the streets.

"Where does your editor get his information from?" asked Course Tutor. "Your photos were unusually good."

He had insisted on a by-line.

"Who else could have taken them?"

Discipulum's coverage of the Grosvenor Square demonstration was singled out at the Student Journalist's Conference that spring.

"First class editorial and pictures," the judges said.

Richard Neville, editor of "Oz", the UK's most recent underground press arrival, was a guest speaker.

There was an audible intake of breath when he swished in.

Ben watched him carefully.

He wondered how much Browncoat already had on file.

Hazel was agitated.

"I thought I might be pregnant."

His body tensed.

"Relax. I've had my period."

"You're not on the pill?"

She shook her head.

"You said you were."

His head thumped back on his pillow.

"Jesus Fucking Christ."

He felt betrayed.

She was wary now.

Tried to kiss him.

He bit her tongue.

"Bastard," she said.

"Not as big a bastard as you."

She knew it was over.

"I wanted to marry you."

He thought he'd had a lucky escape.

"You can look forward to a degree," said Course Tutor. "I'd expect a 2:1.

"Have you begun to look for a job? Photo-journalism perhaps?

"A PhD? We liked your approach to Hardy."

But Ben had had enough. City life was not for him. And a clean sheet was attractive.

"Australia's big and empty," said Daryl.

"You could emigrate. Cost just £10 if they accept you."

The clerk at Australia House was impressed with his degree.

"A graduate can get just about any job they want."

"I'd like something rural. With cattle perhaps?"

"English degrees aren't much use in the outback."

"Can you ride a horse?

Ben nodded.

"There's always work for a jackaroo."

He lifted an eyebrow.

"Station hands who muster cattle on horseback. Expected to turn their hands to just about everything else as well."

Could this be his fresh start?

"I'll be a jackaroo."

His passport would be checked, he would have to be vaccinated, and he would pay £10.

If there were no hitches there would be a seat for him on a flight to Sydney in January.

He left his bedsit and returned to Whiteside.

CHAPTER EIGHT

Catherine likes horses

"Got any more books?" said Tom.

Ben dug out "Room at the Top", "Uses of Literacy" and "A Kind of Loving".

"Hoggart's too old for you so keep him for later. Lots of life lessons in the others though."

"Like what?" said Catherine.

He looked at her. Still black haired, still green-eyed, and about to become beautiful.

He wanted to say "beware of soft eyed women" but offered "it's best to be careful" instead.

"How's Sixth Form?" he added.

"Touchy subject," said Alice. "She's horse mad. Thinks being a groom makes more sense than getting a degree."

"Mam and Dad would like to see you."

That pleased him.

He walked to Tot Swinburne's farm at Great Gables next day.

Dozens of Black and White cows were spread over a thirty-acre field.

Steel framed buildings towered over a squat rectangle of old-fashioned byres.

Meg and Kit's cottage, south facing and framed by oak and elm, was sheltered and neat.

A flower garden in front, vegetable garden to the side, a living room, tiny scullery, and two bedrooms.

A fitted carpet smothered the living room floor.

A vase of fresh flowers softened its single window.

The range was ceramic. A hob, a single oven and a shelf to warm plates.

He recognised photos on the mantelpiece, the cloth on the table, and the cushions that covered its seats.

Kit was in his rocking chair. He still wore ankle high hob nail boots.

Meg's hair was still in a bun.

And a kettle was coming to the boil.

Cheese scones, currant scones and ginger biscuits had been arranged immaculately on spotless floral plates.

She had been a domestic servant on Crown Lane before she married Kit. Her training showed.

"Australia's a long way off," said Meg.

Each of them had seen older relatives leave, gone for ever, to Canada, New Zealand or the United States, when they were young, and times were hard.

They were worried they would not see him again.

"The world's not as big as it was. I'm flying out. It'll take less than two days. What's happening with Catherine?"

"She likes horses," said Kit. "Can't blame her for that."

"She's a very good rider," said Meg. "Keeps winning cups and shields."

Her tone sharpened.

"Fearless. Scared of nothing that one. I'm worried she could get hurt."

"Do you see much of Tom?"

"Lovely boy," said Kit. "Very quiet."

"I had an uncle just like him," said Meg. "He'd spend hours in the woods watching squirrels and birds. Would ride to Whiteside on his milk cow."

She did not tell him she'd had a cousin in Pennsylvania who had been killed in a suspicious car accident during Prohibition with a woman who was not his wife in the passenger seat and the back packed full of bootleg liquor.

***

Henderson and Jim were drawing fat lambs at Wheelstones.

He pushed the stragglers into the race where Henderson checked the cover over their loins and Jim swung the shedding gate.

He whistled up a new dog called Don and walked those not yet ready for market back to Middle Paisley to graze.

It was under a four-year rye grass ley and would be ploughed out in twelve months' time.

When it was being farmed by Kit the wildflower seed heads that flicked his boots each autumn had rattled like castanets.

This time spent dandelion, and an occasional rusting dock, were the only intruders.

"Waltzing Matilda," said Pat when he came in for dinner.

She heaped his plate while he looked round.

The oil-fired Aga was a shock.

And two of the walls in what had been the pantry were punctured by windows with radiators hung beneath.

Seats, and a sofa, were lined in front of a television. A low table was heaped with newspapers and magazines.

"It's a great place to sit," said Jim.

He looked at Pat.

"As long as I take my overalls off first."

She smiled.

"It's so warm. I couldn't have lived with that big black thing."

"What's a jackeroo?" said Jim.

"A farm worker who does a bit of everything and is usually sitting on a horse," he replied.

"Bit of a waste for a Bachelor of Arts," said Henderson.

Ben's head lifted.

"Perhaps it was studying that was the waste of time?"

His uncle frowned.

It was not like Ben to be touchy.

"I'll be no good in Australia unless I'm comfortable on a horse," he said. "Where can I find one?"

Edward looked at him strangely.

"It's Catherine you should be asking. Not me."

"Catherine?"

"Josh's long gone. She rides out point-to-pointers for the Lutton Hall Golightlys at weekends. You'll need something at least seventeen hands. If she can't sniff one out, she'll know someone who can."

Mrs Golightly pulled up outside the Post Office.

"Good morning, Benjamin. How nice to see you," she said as she shook his hand.

He remembered she was Morvale Pony Club's District Commissioner.

She and Catherine chattered about her horses on the drive over.

Oscar had gone lame, nothing serious. Shannon and Petra were coming on well.

Her yard was busy.

He walked with them down a line of boxes.

"This is poor Oscar," said Mrs Golightly, patting his neck.

Catherine was more interested in Shannon.

"She's still green," she told him. "Tried to tank off with me last time out."

Shannon, built for speed, was a fine-looking bay.

"Warm her up in the paddock," said Mrs Golightly. "Jamie will be ready to ride with you when you get back."

"You're looking for a mount, Benjamin," she said when Shannon and Petra had moved off.

She gauged his weight.

"Have to be seventeen hands."

She tapped a riding boot with her crop.

"Outright purchase or weekly hire?"

"Hire makes sense."

"Where would it be stabled?"

"Earthly Mires would be best."

She nodded.

"I might have one."

Max, seventeen hands, ten years old, and a proven hunter, was grazing in a loafing paddock.

"He's sound," said Mrs Golightly. "Let's ride him out and see what you think."

When he hauled himself into the saddle, he felt uneasy.

The neck in front of him stretched for ever and he was a long way off the ground.

"You'll make a handsome pair," said Mrs Golightly who had saddled a grey. "Let's go round the block."

Max was as steady as his ten birthdays suggested. He did not flinch at passing traffic and was soft mouthed as well.

Ben almost giggled when he pushed him into a trot.

The horse's long stride felt awkward and his rhythm was unusually slow. But when he pressed with both knees they spanked along.

He laughed out loud. There was wind in his face and Max had still to move into canter.

Catherine was defensive.

"I won't be a groom for ever."

"Marry a Duke, ride his horses, and have someone else look after them instead?" said Ben.

They were in the back room at The Comet.

She looked at him sideways.

"Horses are big business. I can make them my career."

"What about your "A" levels?"

"I'll get them."

"What'll you do then?"

"Work full time at Lutton Hall. Learn as much as I can. Grab whatever turns up next."

He got the go-ahead from Australia House.

He could leave as scheduled if he topped up his vaccinations first.

He'd stood in queues at school to be inoculated against smallpox, diptheria, whooping cough, tetanus, TB and polio.

It was not a problem to be jabbed for yellow fever, cholera and typhoid as well.

He applied for a Provisional Driving Licence.

Daryl had told him that if he produced one the Aussies would think he'd passed his driving test.

"You could buy a car and get straight into it. You'd have to put on Provisional plates and drive at no more than forty for a year but that would be it."

Scott told him to get his teeth checked. "Australian dentists cost money."

He crammed four new fillings in one Monday and five the next.

Long, low hills stood above them.

"We're going onto the tops today," said Field Master.

Ben, Alf, Edward, Mrs Golightly and Catherine settled into a long uphill trot.

Hounds, a tide of probing noses and thrashing sterns, followed the huntsman who led the way.

Clouds were high, the sky was blue and there was only a whisper of wind.

They moved onto Wenside to watch.

A distant Morton curled in shining loops.

The Ender, deep in its almost parallel valley, glittered.

Fields next to the rivers were pale green.

The grass they were standing in was either coarse brown or weak yellow.

Hounds, heads down, and in open view, raked both sides of the slopes.

Field Master led the way to a smooth crest fringed with steep, concentric gullies.

Ben felt he and Max were surfing as they pushed through them to the summit.

"What are these?" said Catherine.

"Defensive ditches," said Alf. "It's an Iron Age fort."

His arm swept over the bare hillsides.

"I never did work out what they did for water."

The hounds foraged but scented nothing.

Huntsman encouraged them to continue raking either side of the crest.

"Which way will he run if they find?" said Edward.

A line of cars was parked on a track below.

Catherine pointed. "That's Grandad's."

A bitch whimpered. The pack immediately zeroed in.

Its casts became urgent. Others began to yelp, squeak and whine as they passed messages amongst themselves.

Suddenly, with instant co-ordination, they streamed towards the Ender.

"Full cry," said Field Master as he swung his horse downhill, leaned back, and settled into a slow, jerky, canter.

"My nose on your tail," Catherine warned Ben as they followed on.

Riding immediately behind Max was the best way to hold Shannon in.

They hurdled a stream, moved up a short slope, then headed downhill again.

Field Master jumped off a terrace, turned suddenly right, and settled into a comfortable canter.

They were moving, surprisingly easily, along a wide grassed bench that swung through a series of spurs.

"What is this?" yelled Ben to no one in particular.

"The Street," said Mrs Golightly.

"Roman road," Alf added.

Everyone wanted that long, smooth ride to last for ever.

CHAPTER NINE

Yer'd better rattle yer dags

The immigration official who had met him at Kingsford Smith Airport dropped him off at a crowded hostel where he was told 'Robin' would interview him next morning. He was given coupons for a Chinese restaurant and slept on a mattress in a cubicle under some stairs.

Robyn was both businesslike and female. There was work for him on Walrooba Station in New England and he had no second choice.

He caught a train to Armidale next morning where he was picked up by the Station Manager's wife.

"It's two hours to Wally so sit back. Enjoy the ride."

Most of the journey was on corrugated dirt roads.

"Trick is to hit forty miles an hour and skim the top."

A plume of dust trailed their station wagon.

"We could do with some rain."

He ate with them that evening.

She filled his plate with sheep's brains and repeatedly played a ballad that recorded the foolishness of "Tommy the Pommy Jackeroo" on her record player.

His first job was to clean her kitchen grease trap.

The chamber, two feet deep, and two feet below the drain, had filled with rotting scum.

He scooped it out by hand and scalded the unit clean.

The stink lingered on his skin and in his hair for days.

Merino wethers stood in a pen outside a shed with a freshly hosed concrete floor.

They were the biggest sheep he'd seen.

Their legs were longer than a calf's and their bodies were draped in long, woollen skirts.

"We kill and dress five every Thursday," said Station Manager.

"Carcases hang overnight and we joint them first thing Friday mornings."

"Leo," he gestured towards an Aborigine who was Ben's age, "will show you the ropes. After that the job's yours."

"Done this before?" asked Leo.

He did not seem surprised when Ben shook his head.

"Catch one, bring it in here, and don't let go."

Leo held the sheep down with his left knee between its hip bone and its ribs, his right knee across its shoulder, and used a stiletto to cut its throat.

"Got to bleed them out before you skin them, and they die quicker if you do this."

Blood was pulsing as he dragged the severed head back until the neck vertebrae parted and a section of spinal cord was exposed.

"Just needs a nick."

His wrist flicked and the wether shuddered.

"Now it's your turn."

Ben hefted in a second sheep, held it down, stabbed the knife in, then sawed through windpipe, jugular and skin to release it.

The blade was unusually sharp but it was still tough going.

The effectiveness of the cut to the spinal cord pleased him. A single, body length, shiver confirmed the wether had died immediately.

Leo showed him how to skin, paunch and dress.

When Ben tried it took him almost an hour.

His second attempt was not much faster.

"I'll come again next week." said Leo. "But yer'd better rattle yer dags because after that yer on yer own."

Next morning the station hands cut out leg joints and a mountain of chops.

Leo's wife took most of them to the cook house.

Almost everything else, including shoulders, was thrown to a circle of kelpies and blue heelers.

"This is Matey," said Station Manager. "Saddle him. Let's see how you get on."

Matey was fifteen hands, not much more than a pony, but strong.

His saddle had knee cantles. He had not seen them before.

"They hold you in. Stop you going over the top when he slams on the brakes."

It was impossible to trot in a stock saddle.

"Stock horses either walk or canter."

They moved into the yards to try Matey out.

The horse was nimble. He neck reined and his response to knee pressure was immediate.

He could swing through 180 degrees then hit canter from a standing start.

Ben began to enjoy himself.

Each evening they brought in four cows and calves.

The calves were penned for the night and their mothers let back out.

He hand-milked them each morning, released their calves. carried the milk to the cook house and sat down to a breakfast of breaded chops.

"The boundary fence must be ridden each week," said Leo.

"I'm to go with you until you get the hang."

Wire strainers, pliers, hammers, staples, nails, wire netting and coils of wire were either pushed into, or tied onto, saddle packs, then they rode off.

The Tablelands, yellow under a mat of long, sun-dried grass rolled before them.

Gum trees stood in occasional clumps.

Wide paddocks dotted with white headed cattle stretched to the horizon.

Ramparts of rounded stone crowned infrequent humps.

A pair of kangaroos bounded off. The contrast between their huge hind legs and tiny front paws was startling.

So was the length of their extraordinary leaps.

Leo appeared not to notice. His eyes were on the fence.

"Rabbits are big problem. Walrooba not got none and we gotta keep 'em out."

He pointed to a hole that had been forced through the ring of wire netting that surrounded the station.

They dismounted. Leo showed him how to cut out a patch and tie it in.

"Was it a rabbit?" said Ben.

"It was this fella."

Leo pointed to a pangolin, a spiny ant eater, curled protectively just feet away.

It was an ancient animal, like the landscape, its tiny head, long body and huge tail were protected by dragon-like overlapping scales.

He picked it up and dropped it on the non-Walrooba side of the fence.

Ben presented his British Provisional Driving Licence at the police station in Dambally and walked out with an Australian one.

Only one car on show at the garage, a worn FJ Holden saloon with a column gear change, was in his price range.

"It's got track rods," the salesman insisted.

That meant an unusually deep rut was less likely to break a suspension spring.

He took it on a jerky test drive to the top of Main Street but did not stall.

Salesman wanted cash so he walked to the ANZ Bank to get it.

And could not resist calling in at a general store to buy a pair of RM Williams station boots on the way back.

He tied on his "P" plates and waved at the group of mechanics who, eager for entertainment, had gathered to watch him leave.

He drove to Moree that Sunday.

It stood at the foot of the Tablelands.

He wanted to glimpse the Great Australian Plain and the outback that lay beyond.

As soon as he left the town the road became relentlessly straight and endlessly long.

Every creek bed was dry. They looked like they hadn't carried water for months.

He pulled in under a weary gum.

A crow croaked harshly. Again, and then again.

There was no other sign of life. Not even traffic.

He drove on, pulled up, and got out.

Nothing had changed.

The creek beds remained resolutely dry.

And the only thing that moved was another lonely crow.

He turned back.

He would have to travel for days to reach the real outback but already knew inland Australia offered no attraction.

There was a plus side.

When he parked outside the bunkhouse at Walrooba his driving was half decent.

Matey was a good horse.

He no longer saddled him to bring in the milk cows but rode bareback instead.

There was a wicket gate between their paddocks.

Matey went through at full gallop – the posts just inches from his knees.

The horse liked to hurdle the thickest grass tussocks for fun.

He let him do that too.

His milking had become as practised as Old Kit's.

And he could kill and dress five wethers in little more than two hours as well.

"We're mustering for weaning and branding tomorrow," said Station Manager.

"I want you saddled by eight."

He thought he'd been born for cattle work.

The long detour to get behind the herd, the repeated casting to gather each pair, then push them towards the main mob, was exciting.

The endless bellowing as cow called calf, or calf called cow, the dust, the popping of stock whips, the scamper to head off breakaways, and the delicacy with which the milling herd was teased through paddock gates or into a holding pen, was deeply satisfying.

Matey knew the job better than he did.

There were occasions when all he had to do was sit still.

The horse was good at yard work too. Could separate a cow and calf long enough for another rider to ease the cow safely through a gate.

Sometimes he helped to take cows to a distant paddock where they could bawl for their missing calves unheard.

On others he pushed calves through the chute to be branded. Or drafted steers and heifers into separate pens.

His workmates relaxed too.

After yet another evening meal of breaded mutton chops, they sat back in their armchairs and promised to have a hell of a night on the beer when weaning was finished.

"You as well, Ben. Whaddyareckon?"

Walrooba was managed by Macarunda Cattle Pty Ltd whose head office was in Sydney.

The company owned scores of stations across New South Wales, South Australia, and Queensland.

Its executives, polished men wearing suburban clothing, often arrived in a single engine plane that landed on a grass strip in the station's most suitable paddock.

They had to be picked up by car and if a plane waggled its wings as it flew over the station it signalled someone would be waiting.

Ben was cleaning saddles when Mrs Station Manager rushed up.

"Sam's stuck in Dambally. Can you pick Mr Stevens up at the strip?"

He was sitting under a Cessna's wing.

When Ben put his case in the Holden's boot he was amused.

"What's a new chum doing with his own car?" he asked as he settled into the front seat with his briefcase.

Ben dressed wethers that afternoon. A message was waiting when he finished.

Stevens wanted to see him after he'd eaten. He was at Station Manager's house.

"Let's go into the office," he said.

He opened a refrigerator where cans of beer fought with cattle vaccine for space.

"What would you like?"

"Four-X," said Ben.

Stevens was curious.

"What brought you here?"

It was a long evening.

When they'd cleaned out the beer they moved onto Bundaberg rum.

Next day he rode the boundary fence with more to think about than a hangover.

Stevens wanted to establish new stations in Pagamba. Cattle could be its next big thing.

Was he up for it?

Would he go to Sydney to be briefed?

The Pacific island lay above Australia, its reputation was wild and woolly, and it promised more than a new job.

Its bush, and the opportunities it offered, were endless.

He and Matey dropped into a shallow gulley.

A section of fence had been smashed.

He wrestled with wire and strainers, but new posts were needed, and the repair was makeshift.

He was about to get on Matey when a huge kangaroo hopped out from behind some gums.

They stared at each other.

They were the same height. His head was sheep-like. Every one of his features enormous. Even his front legs were muscled.

He was so close Ben could see urine stains beneath his penis.

It was still studying him when he rode off.

CHAPTER TEN

Make camp. Get water. Make fire

Stevens, neat in his Sydney uniform of short-sleeved white shirt, neatly ironed shorts, long socks, and polished shoes was sitting on his desk when Ben came in.

His legs had been tanned a pleasant brown. Ben's, only just exposed to sun in his first shorts since First Form, were shocking pink.

A relief map of Pagamba dominated one of the office walls.

It confirmed a mountain landscape sliced by wide river valleys.

A smattering of red markers highlighted the handful of Macarunda stations that had already been established. The deep interior was flag free.

He stood in front of it and called him over.

"We want to run many more cattle in Pagamba. Most of its river valleys have grazing but breeding females are scarce and it costs too much to ship stock in."

"However," he looked directly at Ben, "there could be hundreds ready to be collected right here."

His forefinger traced a thin line along Pagamba's coast.

"Their principal function is to keep copra plantations tidy, but management is poor and most herds are the scungiest I've seen.

"If we crossed those females with Australian bulls we could use their heifer calves as the foundation for new herds.

"First job is to move those within range from A to B."

"From the coast to here or here," he said, pointing to the red flags.

"Are you up for it?"

The flight from Sydney to Pagamba's capital city took five hours.

A second, in a four-seater plane with just one engine, to its north coast took almost two.

Next day he drove to Shantata Plantation to look over his first mob of scrub cattle.

Dozens of bare-chested men wearing only shorts or long cloth skirts, had spread out under a canopy of palms to collect, and de-husk, fallen coconuts.

A multi-coloured herd grazed beyond them.

"They can't gather the nuts if they can't see 'em," explained a potbellied man, with a toothbrush moustache, who was wearing a slouch hat and unusually long shorts. "Cattle keep the grass short but they breed like flies. That's why we've got so many."

Stevens was right when he'd said the stock would be poor quality.

Not all the males had been castrated which meant son could ride mother and brother hop onto sister. In-breeding must have persisted for generations. It was no surprise the entire herd was stunted.

The veranda surrounding Shantata's bungalow was cool.

A house servant offered beer or tea.

Ben chose tea, asked for eighty females, nominated a price well below Stevens' top line, and said he'd select them.

Toothbrush Tash was delighted.

Tried to press a beer on him to celebrate but failed.

"I need someone who can pull together a labour line and walk eighty cattle from Shantata to Kintausi," he told a circle of sunburned men, the same age as himself, who were sitting under a patio umbrella, directly above a narrow beach and a shifting sea.

Their twelve-ounce stubbies had been slotted into polystyrene coolers and Ben had already been chided for leaving his bottle unprotected.

"You shouldn't be drinking warm beer, mate."

They looked at each other. A couple were field officers who routinely visited outlying villages to update electoral registers, another checked out bush people for leprosy or yaws, and the remainder either maintained roads, or constructed new ones.

"It'd be at least five nights. No roads. Bush all the way," said one.

"How're you gonna cross the Ikomo?" asked another.

The others shook their heads, studied the surf, and sipped their beer.

A bare-chested waiter asked if more was needed.

"Your shout, Rod," said Warm Beer Advisor.

"Seven stubbies, my tab, and be quick," said Rod.

They drank their beer in silence.

"What's Greg Schuster doing?" asked one.

"Driving a bulldozer for Public Highways at Manoko," said another.

Warm Beer Advisor turned to Ben. "He's your man if the money's good enough."

"Kua's my boss-line. He'll keep things moving," said Schuster.

Kua, who was barefoot, had a huge chest and a black beard.

"That straight, Mr Greg," he said. "Me got six good fellow help man. They here morning."

Ben had drafted eighty females. All un-bred heifers.

They were standing in a holding pen looking puny and dejected. Every one of their ribs showed.

"They're good," said Schuster. "The lighter they are the easier they'll be to wrestle with when we get to the Ikomo."

All six good fellows had arrived carrying an axe, a bush knife, and a net shoulder bag.

He and Ben would carry ex-army rucksacks with sheet sleeping bags, mosquito nets, a change of clothes, porridge oats and tins of peaches.

A metal box that held a sack of brown rice, tins of Japanese mackerel, Australian corned beef, more mosquito nets, and a dozen head halters, had been tied to a pole that would be hefted by two men.

"All make change-change," said Kua.

"Everyone will take a turn," Greg explained.

One man would shoulder a rolled canvas sheet.

Another would lug cooking pots, a bucket, and plastic water containers that swung from two paddle-shaped sticks.

The cattle, which were trained to be led instead of driven, followed Kua, off the plantation into the bush.

"She's the boss-cow," said Greg pointing to a white heifer that had pushed to the front.

"If she goes forward the rest will follow. We'll only get problems if Whitey there's asked to do something she doesn't want to."

Kua's bush knife swung almost continually at vines and creepers. He occasionally stopped to hack through a low branch.

They walked until they reached a wide patch of coarse grass in mid-afternoon.

"It'll do," said Greg.

He turned to Kua.

"Make camp. Get water. Make fire."

Then to Ben.

"I didn't have to tell him that. He knows the routine better than I do."

Ben watched as saplings with a "Y" fork at one end, that had been trimmed to a point at the other, were driven into the ground to make posts.

Approved as other poles were lain across them and tied down with vine ropes.

And joined the group effort to hoist the canvas over the frame to make a low shelter.

The meal was communal with everyone spooning boiled rice and canned meat onto their tin plate.

Someone had found wild papayas.

"Best to call them paw-paw or no-one will know what you're talking about," said Greg, scooping out seeds which he threw on the fire.

Each of them slept under his mosquito net.

And someone kept feeding the fire with damp wood so the mosquitos, that had whined a thin, unrelenting chorus throughout the night, were further discouraged by smoke.

Kua boiled water while it was still dark.

Breakfast was porridge, tinned peaches, and tea.

"We move at first light. If you want to shit you drop your keks somewhere out there," said Greg, waving an arm. "If you need toilet paper it's in the box."

He handed Ben a large root that had been cooked in the ashes of the fire.

"It's taro. Just starch. Tastes of nothing. But unless we find more paw-paw, or some mangoes, there won't be anything else to eat before we make camp."

Whitey followed Kua as soon as he moved off.

Ben watched Greg splash his face when they forded a small river.

"We'll hit the Darra soon. It comes straight out of the mountains so it's cool. You can give yourself a proper wash then," he said.

The river was fast and deep.

The cattle crossed it in line – standing upstream of each other in an unbroken chain so each of them half covered the animal below.

"Instinct," said Greg. "They do it to protect each other from the full current, and none of this mob'll have crossed a river before."

The herd had been pushed downstream and left the Darra fifty yards lower than it went in.

Kua had stopped walking and was hacking excitedly at a rotten tree trunk.

"That's it for half an hour," said Greg. "Won't be able to drag them past it."

The others joined in. Their axes swung, wood chips flew, and every so often one would cram something into his mouth.

He called Kua who grinned as he came over and opened his palm to show a pulsating wood grub almost the size of his little finger.

"Witchetty," said Greg. "You'll have to eat it."

Kua nipped off its head.

Ben steeled himself, crunched, and filled his mouth with cream.

It was surprisingly easy to swallow.

"We'll cook some later. You'll have eaten scampi? Toasted witchetty's even better," Greg promised.

"Village people forage when they're in the bush. Can live off the land if they have to. Eat just about anything that fits into a pot."

"You've smelt their tobacco. That's wild. They gather what they can and dry it as they go. I encourage them to keep re-stocking their pantry. If you look after your line, they'll look after you."

Ben's heart sank when they reached the Ikomo.

It was at least four hundred yards wide and its currents swirled.

They had made camp half a mile above a mid-stream gravel bank when Greg ran through his plan.

"We'll have to halter them individually to take them over. Everyone taking their turn."

"If we go in here we should be able to get onto the gravel where we can rest. Lot depends on how deep the water is."

"The second leg will be tricky 'cause they'll have to swim. We'll chop out a canoe so we can push them sideways. Across the current."

A crush was built so each animal could be haltered.

A light log was chipped into a crude canoe.

Eight heifers were pushed into the crush and haltered.

When Whitey was led to the river she put her head down, planted her front feet, and refused to move.

Ben prodded her with a pointed stick.

She jumped forward three feet and stood again.

Ben prodded, Whitey jumped, and she eventually stood in the river.

"One last poke and wish me luck," said Greg.

He was holding the downstream side of her head and fought to keep her moving across the current.

They reached the top side of the gravel bank as planned.

"Me now," said Kua.

He wrestled his way over too.

Ben was last. His height was an advantage. He could brace his feet on the riverbed and lean away from his heifer's flailing front legs.

Even so he was wondering how long he could last the pace when they staggered out.

Kua and Kombil returned to pick up the canoe.

"Round two," said Greg.

Kua was already in position.

It was easier to nudge a heifer across the current if she was swimming.

Greg waved when he and Whitey got over.

Kua and Kombil shuttled to and fro.

All eight heifers won through.

"They can look after themselves," said Greg.

They walked a mile upstream and waded back over.

"We'll try for four, maybe five, crossings a day," said Greg, "and take turns on the canoe."

"What's this?" Ben asked.

They'd eaten and were getting ready to duck inside their nets.

He pointed to an angry scratch on his leg. Nothing special except it was leaking pus.

"Tropical ulcer," explained Greg. "Worse for new arrivals than they are for us.

"For a month, maybe two, just about all your cuts will get infected."

He rummaged in the metal box and came back with a bottle, a lint pad, and a bandage.

He poured thick, yellow liquid onto the lint and clamped it on Ben's leg.

"Acriflavine emulsion. It'll suck the shit out. Hold the pad while I fix the dressing."

After the last heifer had been manhandled across, they pushed their gear over on a raft.

And when a new camp had been built Greg declared the next day was Sunday.

"We need to rest."

He and Ben were sitting on a flat rock with their feet in the river.

"Kintausi'll be a good station."

"Good pasture. Good manager. Airstrip close by. But a bad neighbour."

"The Sacred Mission of the Risen Christ. One of the new sects from America. Total dopes and a complete pain in the arse."

He looked at Ben.

"They'll be down the moment they see you. Warn you to keep away from women and invite you to join them at Bible class to make sure of your salvation."

He looked at Ben again.

"Not joking, mate."

CHAPTER ELEVEN

Me line-cook now

When he returned to Kintausi with a third batch of scrub heifers, his legs and arms were thick with tropical ulcers.

Each of them a red scratch with a green middle that was nothing on its own, but their combined malevolence had hatched lumps in both armpits and each side of his groin.

Acriflavine was not enough to suppress their fretwork of increasingly angry lines.

"You'll have to darken Risen Christ's hospital door," said Kintausi's manager.

Ben was reluctant.

Pastor Sebastian had, as Greg had warned, descended within hours of the Shintata cattle coming in.

He was a thin, intense man. Perhaps just eight stones with an evangelist's bushy beard and piercing blue eyes.

"Welcome to Kintausi, my Brother in Christ. We share God's perfect kingdom. May His will be done."

He'd tried to bear hug Ben but when he'd stepped back the blue eyes had flared.

"God loves everyone. Even sinners. Let us embrace in His name," said Sebastian.

Ben had shaken his head.

"Come, my brother. His son. Repentance lifts the soul. The doors of our church are always open."

Ben had stepped back again.

"Mary is the virgin mother of the Risen Christ," Sebastian, eyes sparking, had said as he left.

"All women are holy and the sin of lechery shall not befoul them."

Sister Perfecta may have worn a crucifix, and a wimple, but she was also a nurse.

"Injection first," she said, priming a syringe with penicillin.

"Three ccs now and two more over consecutive days. You must not miss them.

"You don't have to pull your pants right down. Just halfway."

She stood back and studied his limbs.

Each ulcer would have to be dressed separately.

"Shirt off. Boots off."

There were infected scratches the length of each arm, the back of his neck, across his shoulders and down both legs.

"Hilda will dress one side and I'll do the other."

Hilda was in nurse's uniform.

She had dark skin and her focus was intense.

Hilda gave him his second injection and helped to change his dressings on the third day.

The pus had gone. Perfecta replaced acriflavine with antiseptic cream.

"That should be enough," she said. "They'll soon be healed."

"You've had a haircut," said Hilda as he left.

His fourth cattle trip, bringing in another mob of eighty or so maiden heifers, had crossed a range of mountains.

He'd bought a shotgun and his labour line ate pigeon.

He liked it in the hills. It was cooler and there was less infection.

When he got back there was a party in the Macarunda compound.

Station Manager had loaned his record player.

Elvis Presley alternated with Slim Dusty and the social club throbbed.

Hilda was pleased to see him.

She waved when he ducked through the door.

Careless of who heard her, she shouted, "Whose face is that?"

He'd just begun to talk to her when Pastor Sebastian burst in.

"Music is a tool of Satan. Dancing is a gateway to the eternal fires of Hell."

Somone switched off the record player. Others hid in the kitchen.

"You," thundered Sebastian pointing at Hilda. "You Magdalen. How dare you stain the mantle of the Holy Mother by making union within this assembly of the iniquitous, the adulterous and thieves? Get out!"

Hilda shrank.

Ben continued to stand beside her.

"It's you who should not be here, Pastor Sebastian."

The silence that followed was absolute.

Hell's infernos could not have blazed more furiously than Sebastian's eyes when he turned to go.

"There's a village below the Kwishebe mountains that's been running a herd of pedigree Santa Gertrudis for six years," said Station Manager. "Same old story. The stock bull's shagging his daughters and three of his sons are playing leapfrog with their sisters and mothers. The Department of Agriculture says we can take all four bulls as long as we swap them with one of our Brahmans."

"Just four?"

Station Manager laughed.

"They had an urgent lesson in castration three years ago."

Ben passed word out for Diman, his boss-line.

"Where Kwinika?" he asked.

Diman's eyebrows lifted.

"It strange place."

"You know road?"

"Tori know. His mama belong there."

Ben whistled up his labour line. They picked out a quiet young bull, and two old cows to keep him company while they travelled.

Tori assured him the route was good.

"Track all way. Go up Kwishebe. Down Kwinika. Four night? Five night something?"

They set off next day.

"Mr Ben," said Diman.

"Someone follow. Think Hilda."

She was barefoot, a large net bag hung down her back, and she spoke in bush patois.

"Me line-cook now."

She did not try to single him out.

She cooked for everyone, joined the fireside gossip, shared the canvas shelter at night, and bargained when villagers offered fresh fruit or vegetables.

The bull astonished her.

"Why he lazy? Let cow walk front. That man work."

Ben tried to explain that heavy bulls preferred more nimble lead cows to gauge risk.

Kwinika was tucked inside a wide river's loop.

The headman was pleased with his huge, heavily dewlapped, almost black, new bull.

He asked if he could keep the cows too.

Ben looked over his cattle.

The Santa Gertrudis bulls, red and much smoother than massively humped Brahmans, were striking.

He'd make up his mind about leaving the cows later.

When he got back to the village he asked for his spare clothes.

Diman pointed to a hut set on stilts.

"They up that."

He climbed the ladder.

"Hello Ben," she said. "I'm very clean. I washed in the river."

She pressed her nose against his.

"Now we will lie down together."

They ate on a low platform with the headman, his family, Diman and the line.

Fresh fish, boiled pumpkin, and baked yam.

"That good," said Hilda, patting her tummy.

Ben bargained with the headman.

He'd swap one cow for two bullocks.

The headman, who recognised the value of a breeding female over animals that had been neutered, tried hard to hide his smile.

Next morning they mustered the herd and drafted the stock for Kintausi.

Ben asked the headman to hold his cattle till midday.

Then told Diman to push their small group as far and as fast as he could.

He did not want them to hear their herd mates returning to pasture and turn back to join them.

Hilda adopted her old role on the way back.

She cooked, slept in a corner, and kept away from the bulls.

It was an easy journey.

The paths were clear, the rivers shallow, and the cattle obedient.

Station Manager was pleased with the bullocks.

"I'm fed up with frozen meat."

He looked at Ben.

"You'll want a double bed for your donga?"

She was straightforwardly direct. Could not be coquette, flippant, or dizzy.

She was unrelentingly physical too. She had to touch him.

An arm over his shoulder or a hand on top of his own.

When they sat together she always put an ankle over his.

Nor could she hide her feelings.

If he'd been annoying she cuffed his shoulder – "you stupid man".

Or smacked his forearm – "don't be silly".

But other times she'd rub her cheek against his or kiss the back of his neck.

She owned him.

Station Manager and Ben had picked the biggest bullock.

It would be killed, cut, and distributed the following day.

He'd sharpened the best knives he could find, asked Diman to do the same with his axe, and cut out a cross-tree.

"We'll put up a pulley and hang him from here," said Ben, pointing to a beam above a workshop door.

"Catch his guts on a tarpaulin."

"We'll need buckets for the blood as well."

Station Manager rubbed his chin.

"Have you done this before?"

"Only with sheep."

"Can you cut joints. Separate rump steak from topside?"

"I'll try."

"Do you see any problems?"

"One big one. Can we get it into fridges before it goes off?

"Have you any suggestions?"

"Keep it simple by mincing the forequarter. And offer everything else except hindquarter cuts to the labour line."

"Everything?"

"The lot. On condition they burn or bury what they don't want and clean up as well."

Ben looked round.

"We need to make a cutting bench. Four kitchen tables covered by old doors?"

He shot the bullock, opened its neck, separated the carotid artery, gestured for the first bucket to be pushed closer, and cut.

Blood poured out. It seemed like gallons. There was a rush to prevent any being spilled.

He moved to the hind legs and sliced between the thigh bone and tendon directly above each hock.

Diman pushed in the cross-tree and tied it to a rope hanging from the pulley.

He and Ben wrestled with the hide for almost an hour before it was laid out to be scraped and dried.

His labour line's families were standing guard over a tarpaulin that was already home to the head, feet, and tail.

The carcase steamed as it swung from the beam.

Ben cut into the abdomen, sawed vigorously, then stepped back as stomachs and intestine spilled out.

He waved to the labour line's wives – "them belong you" – and waited until the mess had been cleared.

Diman took his axe to the breastbone and neck.

The lungs, heart, windpipe and oesophagus were removed.

They were taken by Line Wives too.

The carcase was lowered so Diman could attack the spine.

His axe work was patient. It eventually swung in two halves and was washed down with a hose.

Ben rested as Line Wives stripped out the stomachs and intestines.

Then he glugged down iced water and settled into phase two.

Each side weighed about three hundred pounds.

The station was beginning to be stunned by the volume of fresh meat.

Diman put down a fresh tarpaulin.

He and Ben attacked the forequarters first.

Their knives rasped against the steel as they fought to maintain a cutting edge.

The shoulder bones were enormous.

Ben separated the ribs. Hilda cut out their huge eye muscles. Station Manager's wife stacked the rib eyes then the mincing beef.

Every refrigerator on Kintausi hummed in expectation.

"Now for the tricky bit."

His stiletto laboured as it traced the first hindquarter's topside seam.

And he thought he'd managed to cut out the rump.

The sirloin was more easily defined.

Macarunda staff would barbecue all week.

He sliced out the fillet and gave it to Hilda.

"Can you get that to Perfecta?"

The leg muscles defeated him.

"Put them through a mincer."

Thigh bones, long and polished, joined others on a skeletal heap.

The second hindquarter had still to be jointed.

Line Wives worked hurriedly.

Other station workers waited.

He and Hilda listened to the party after they went to bed.

Laughter swelled, voices rose, and hand drums began to beat.

Someone strummed monotonously on a small guitar.

"They're getting drunk on meat instead of beer," said Hilda.

She knew how good a stomach full of meat could feel.

Ben had been taught to appreciate it too.

Meg had often made ox tail soup.

He'd grumble because his plate was full of bones.

"You have to suck on them. That's how you find the meat."

"And spit them gently onto your spoon when you're finished," she warned.

"Did Perfecta get that steak?" said Ben.

Hilda nodded.

"Pastor Sebastian is a bad man," she said.

Ben knew that.

"He ordered new brassieres for the cook girls and watched them when they were sorting out the right size.

"They had to stand with bare breasts while he stood behind and helped to put them on."

Ben was up on one elbow.

"In his office?"

Hilda nodded.

"He held their breasts, looked at the bra, and told them if it was the right size."

"The bastard," Ben said.

Hilda nodded again.

CHAPTER TWELVE

Betting Blind

Stevens flew in after the Shantata heifers had calved. They had responded to good grazing and filled out.

Most of their calves had brown coats with dark, vertical stripes.

"Brindles," he said. "Who'd have guessed it?"

They were alert too. Ran to their mothers with tails flying and heads high.

"Hybrid vigour's an astonishing thing."

Ben sat in when he and Station Manager discussed development plans.

Kintausi was fully stocked.

Soon it would be supplying other stations with bulling heifers and Pagamba's capital city with fresh beef.

The pros and cons of operating an on-station abattoir and freezer unit were examined.

The airstrip would have to be extended.

Should more bush be cut back to make new paddocks?

Would setting up their own sawmill be a good idea?

"We're planning to move into the central high land," Stevens told Ben. "If you want to manage your own station you should go there."

"My family live in the high land," said Hilda. "My father is head man for the Ongil clan at Komun close to the Bondan river."

"What type of country is it?"

"Where we live it is steep. It is flat, sometimes swampy, by the river. We try to grow coffee. My father has said he'd like to own cattle."

She considered destiny as she lay beside him.

Its twists, blind alleys, and hidden doorways, the strange man whose hand rested on her stomach, and the chance meeting that had put it there.

She threw off their sheet, rolled him over, and stroked his back.

"Why is your bum so white? When I saw it at Risen Christ I thought it was very strange."

"Never gets the sun," said Ben. "Your bum is lighter than your arms and legs as well."

She smacked him across both cheeks.

"That's because you are the only one who sees it."

It was not just his bum that was different.

His eyes were too. They changed so often.

When he was challenged, they stabbed like daggers.

When he was thinking, they became deep pools.

And when he smiled, they smiled as well.

Stevens sat with him in the Highland District Administrator's office at Dagwia.

The map on his desk highlighted villages in red and the Bondan river in blue.

Land immediately either side of the Bondan showed as an unbroken white strip.

"A cattle station would be welcome," said the DA. "Our Department of Agriculture hopes to establish herds in villages along the valley. Infrastructure introduced by Macarunda would be a great help."

Ben was told to scout opportunities out.

When government staff finished work, they headed for Dagwia's Social Club where Ben, armed with a twelve-ounce stubby, was waiting.

They were keen to help. He was told an abandoned coffee plantation just above the Bondan at Ongwa might be interesting.

"A Queenslander leased a huge lump of land, built a bungalow, but couldn't make money so flew back home."

The property was already overgrown. Infant coffee bushes had been choked by resurgent grass, fences sagged, bush had re-invaded the perimeter and the bungalow was smothered by unruly shrubs.

A Field Officer led him onto the veranda. Ben stamped his feet. It was solid.

Its interior was even better.

A large living room, good kitchen, toilet, shower, and two bedrooms. There was a smaller house for a cook. And a shed for a generator.

"Why are these windows so high?"

The sills were six feet off the floor.

"They didn't want local people peeping in."

Stevens gave the go-ahead, Macarunda took over the mortgage and the lease, Ben moved into the house, and Hilda told him the station was just below her village.

When she called on her father he was sitting outside his hut.

"I see you," said Kunjin.

They embraced.

A line of brothers, half-brothers, sisters, half-sisters, uncles, aunts and cousins, gathered to greet her too.

They sat in a circle. Pleased to be together.

Their conversation was light. Births, marriages, deaths, who was absent at school or work, and who was doing what with whom.

More important issues, progress with their coffee, relations with their neighbours, plans for cattle and Hilda's astonishing lift in fortune would be discussed later.

She suggested her father offer clan labour to Ben.

And asked three nephews to help her with the garden.

"We should lower these," she said, pointing to the kitchen and living room windows. "When we are sitting here I want to see outside. The bedroom and bathroom windows can stay as they are."

He agreed.

They went into the garden.

"It could be good. We should keep these," she said, pointing to hibiscus and frangipani. "And plant more.

"And look at these."

Two bamboo clumps whispered and swayed.

"We will sit underneath them.

"The rest is rubbish. It should be cut down and burned. We will grow short grass instead.

"These boys will help."

She pointed to the youths who were waiting, almost hidden, in dappled shadow.

"We'll start now."

He walked Ongwa with Kunjin. He was wondering how many cattle it could carry, where he would find them, where he should put the yards, and if there was room for an airstrip.

Kunjin was stunned at the opportunities offered by Ben's arrival.

"Me get plenty men. They rub out this," he said, pointing to the scrub.

"When get cow they cut this so come up new," he said, waving a hand at the waist-high grass.

"Help make fence?" said Ben.

Kunjin shook his head."

"Not got savvy."

"Help make cow yard?"

"That easy," said Kunjin pointing to the bush. "Them Ongil tree."

"I need boss-line. Go with me bring back cow. Look after cow when cow come here."

"Know good man. He work with Macarunda before. His name Kobe. Bring good men with him."

When Stevens drove in, Ben asked for an outside fencing team and outlined plans for a private airstrip.

"We could graze it, like they did at Walrooba, and take the cattle off when it is being used."

Building a herd was a bigger problem. It could only be assembled piecemeal.

"I've found thirteen breeders that an outlying mission no longer wants and there's another fifteen or so on the fringe of Kwishebe," said Ben.

Stevens wondered whether weaned heifer calves could be flown into Dagwia on short-take-off transports like the Otter or Caribou.

"Have to be hog-tied or stalled. I'll talk to head office."

He liked Hilda's garden – especially the bamboo.

"I'll bring some avocado plants next time. The two older Santa Gertrudis bulls and three bulling heifers could come in from Kintausi."

It took Ben nine days to walk them through.

He bought a Toyota Landcruiser and taught Hilda to drive on the new airstrip.

Dagwia's Police Inspector stamped her licence.

When he was not scouring the countryside for cattle he joined a brag school.

He could still switch on his calculator, and still played to win, but scooping this pot was not easy.

There were never fewer than eight players and most were single men with salaries at least as good as his own.

He identified the reckless, lucky, cautious, shrewd, bold, and those who could not hold their beer, but even though some games continued beyond midnight he was always pleased to break even.

Gossip was a bonus. The men around the table worked as field administrators, for the Department of Agriculture, or on coffee plantations, and they had good ears.

"There's a mongrel herd in the Kumbai," said one.

He found a miserable mob of evangelical Mission in-breds ranging an entire valley and came back with most of the heifers.

"A Catholic Mission at Kinsokora breeds cattle," said another.

He discovered a pair of priests blasting out a new road with gelignite, a well-managed herd of Red Polls, and made immediate arrangements to swap stock bulls regularly and exchange bulling heifers.

Hilda had pulled up outside Dagwia's new clothes store.

"We don't serve boongs," said the Australian behind the counter.

She had thin lips, a lined face, and weary eyes. The outback had sucked her dry.

"What is a boong?"

"One of your kind. Go on. Skedaddle."

Hilda moved to a rack. She picked up a frock, examined the label, and measured it against herself.

"Don't touch them," said Thin Lips who had moved beside her.

She looked as if she was ready to slap Hilda's arm.

"What is my kind?" said Hilda.

"A darkie. A blackfella. A gin."

"I'll have this one," said Hilda, pulling out her money.

She was pleased Thin Lips had taken it because if she had not she would have hit her.

He set off with Kobe to look at cattle in Kwishebe.

Furan Mission had walked its foundation stock in from the other side of the island and had surplus heifers to sell.

It took five nights to get there, he had picked out twenty-five good heifers, but the route back was difficult.

He fixed a price and tried to plan a way through.

Kobe was uneasy.

"These people new," he said. "Not long have government. Still kill each other. Axe? Spear? Arrow? Anything. Do it easy if want to."

Ben was more interested in the narrow, steep-sided Meghi valley.

"We can walk them down there but will have to pull them up. We'll need ropes and ten men."

Kobe agreed.

"I'm coming with you," said Hilda. "Me go line-cook 'gain."

He was pleased. She was good company and he wanted to be able to talk to someone in English.

On his last trek his waking thought one morning, as he geared his mind to review the coming day, had been: "Do what thing now?"

It took two days to get the cattle across the Meghi.

Kobe's labour line was good.

It improvised slings in which the heifers could be lifted, carried, pulled and pushed across the river and up the other side.

Ben looked at their cuts, bruises and blisters and decided to rest when they reached the next river.

"No more cow hide in bush," said Kobe. "Do what thing now?"

"Wait Ongwa cow have baby," said Ben.

He and Hilda sat on a rock and dangled their feet in the water.

"What will you do?" she asked.

"Stocking Ongwa was like building a house. We can bring in more Kintausi heifers next year but until then we'll have done what we can so we'll sit back and enjoy it."

Kunjin took them to a village celebration.

"It will be traditional," said Hilda. "Everyone will be wearing feathers and shells, they will kill many pigs and have a big party while they eat them.

"Like Kintausi after the bullock except there'll be more drums, and more dancing."

Kunjin had exchanged his shirt and shorts for a feather headdress, a shell necklace, thick bark belt, a woven loin cover and a rustling bustle of leaves to cover his backside. He had unusual scars on his left shoulder, his upper left arm and the top of his left leg.

Ben watched as almost a hundred pigs were tied to a line of stakes.

Fires were blazing fiercely under piles of carefully stacked stones.

Open pits had been dug out beside them.

"They are traditional ovens. We heat the stones red hot, line the pit with them, put down banana leaves, put the pig in, heap vegetables on top of it, then more banana leaves, cover them with the rest of the hot stones, put on more banana leaves. then seal it with soil to keep the heat in."

She looked at him anxiously but could read nothing but interest.

"They will take about five hours to cook. Some women will keep an eye on things. Others will dance until the food is ready."

"Would you like to join them?" he asked.

She did.

"I have not brought the right clothes."

He watched as each pig was killed. Most with a single blow to the head.

Their guts were stripped out then each carcase was dragged over an open fire to singe off its hair and placed in the waiting pits.

Kunjin was one of the many men who paraded in front of them, a spear in one hand, his axe in his belt, gesturing expansively and talking loudly.

"We killed many pigs five years ago and invited the people who live here to help us eat them. My father is saying thank you for inviting him to help them eat theirs. Many people from my family are here. We will talk to them later."

The men who danced wore tall headdresses and leaf bustles. Some beat on hand drums. Others faked traditional combat and waved spears.

The women's headdresses were red, their grass skirts yellow, and they were bare chested.

Hilda watched him.

"What are you thinking?"

He could have joked about not knowing tits came in so many shapes and sizes.

"That bras hide their secrets very well."

She laughed, linked arms with him, and rested her head on his shoulder.

He began to win at cards more often. One night he woke Hilda up and emptied his pockets on their bed.

They counted his loot.

"Two hundred and forty dollars," she said. "You are a magician."

"It's ours," he said. "We'll keep it to use later. Invite your father down to see me."

Kunjin waited beneath a bamboo.

Ben sat with him, listened to its wind whisper, and occasional hollow thunk.

Kunjin produced a sheet of newspaper, crumpled a tobacco leaf, and rolled a cigarette.

"We talk pig," said Ben.

Kunjin nodded.

"How people have so many to kill?"

"Have female. They have baby. If not enough buy other."

"Buy how much money?"

"Three hundred dollar, four hundred dollar, maybe more."

Ben was astonished.

"Where get money?"

"Sell coffee bean. Dig new government road. Sell headdress feather."

"How much money this pig?"

He marked a height with his hand that would have covered a 200-pound bacon weight animal back at Whiteside.

Kunjin wrinkled his nose. "Two hundred dollar something."

"How long take grow?" He marked bacon weight height again.

"Two year, three year, something."

It took less than five months at Sunny Banks.

"What they eat?"

"Old sweet potato. Sweet potato leaf. Pumpkin skin. Thing cook woman not want."

One evening the regular Dagwia card game became suddenly serious.

There had been a run of unusually good hands. Some pots were enormous. Gossip stopped. Concentration lifted. No one was going home.

"The cards are hot," said Tim Brewster.

Each dealer distributed his offerings with unusual restraint. Each hand was picked up carefully. Its message expressionlessly read.

The opening bet had lifted to ten dollars. Ben usually went blind for two circuits to build the pot.

Sometimes he stacked immediately. Others he stuck with his hand only to underline that it might be a good one. If a hand that had been blind was played after being picked up it almost always unsettled the table.

Bets had lifted to thirty dollars. He had a good hand so he played on. Then forty. He stuck with that too. Just three players were left. A triangle. A situation that favoured the bold and the lucky.

"Raise you fifty," he said.

There was a rustle. The players who were left were not fools.

"Stack," said Jack Connelly.

"See you" said Paul Tompkin who counted out one hundred dollars.

Ben won.

Play became even more intense. After stacking a couple of times he decided to force the pace.

"Thirty blind."

The odds had not changed. Just the risk.

Eyes hardened. The response was flinty. They knew he was using his winnings to panic them.

He played two more rounds blind then picked up. All his will was focussed on keeping his face expressionless. He was looking at the jack, queen, and king of diamonds. There was only a one in five hundred chance of being beaten.

He let others make the pace. Betting lifted to eighty dollars. Four players were still in. At least one must have a very good hand too.

He decided to test the field.

"One hundred."

Eyes lifted. But everyone stuck with him. None wanted to give in.

"Two hundred."

He still had enough money in front of him to make the bet but if play came round again it was IOU time.

Only one person stacked.

Back to a triangle. And the other players earned more than he did.

"Three hundred."

He wrote an IOU.

Play went round again.

"Four hundred." Another IOU.

Then the balloon burst.

"Stack."

"See you."

And he'd won again.

Everyone leaned back. Pleased to be able to breathe more easily.

"I don't want to know how much is front of you," said Jack Connelly.

Neither did he. He'd count it later.

"One last hand," said Tim Brewster. "Got to have a chance of winning something back."

Ben picked up immediately.

Three fives. A hand so rare it would beat a running flush.

"I'm not betting," he said. "I'll only claim the pot."

He showed his hand.

There were groans.

"Can't believe it," said Brewster.

Connelly was cross. "You shouldn't have done that. Somone might have had better."

"Turn them over and see."

There were even more groans.

Not all their hands were duds but none was better than a run.

"Well done, cattle man," said Bert Fewster. "The quality of mercy is not strained."

Ben stuffed his shirt pockets, then his shorts, and dropped what he could not cram into them down his shirt front.

When he counted it out on his kitchen table there was just short of five thousand dollars.

CHAPTER THIRTEEN

Hilbenkunpit

"Hilda was a star pupil," said the Lutherene Mission pastor. "We hope you are looking after her?"

"I am," said Ben.

The pastor nodded.

"How can I help?"

"Could you introduce me to your farm manager?"

Kris Erickson was a big Norwegian.

"Have you any concrete pens?" said Ben.

Erickson showed him two sheds.

"That's for our hens," he said. "We started with pigs in the other."

It had four sections, each with a concrete floor, access to a front feeding passage, troughs and water bowls.

"What happened?"

"We needed more fruit and vegetables for the hospital. Pigs weren't profitable and competed with them for labour."

"Where did you sell them?"

"Took them to pork weight. That's what the freezer shop in Dagwia wanted. Freighting in their feed was too expensive."

"You sold nothing to local villages?"

Erickson shook his head.

"Could I rent or lease these pens?"

"Not my decision. Pastor Schmidt's the man."

He sat with Schmidt for more than an hour and outlined his proposition.

The German was hard-nosed. Would not consider a fly-by-night operation.

He wanted to see a business plan that had been approved by Macarunda.

He outlined the conditions for a lease as well. They included a permanent, on-site manager.

Stevens was thoughtful.

"There's a lot there. I'll have to think about letting you run a side operation. The site manager would have to be reliable. And how do you overcome the cost of flying in high protein concentrate?"

Hilda was excited.

"It should be Pita," she said emphatically.

Pita, her younger brother, was about to begin his final year at Brisbane University.

"Will he want to work here?" said Ben.

"This is his home."

She called on Pastor Schmidt.

"Would you like to employ a staff nurse?"

He did. He was pleased to see her and asked about Pita's studies.

"We have to be clever," she told Ben. "The Lutherene Mission likes me. If I work there it will be more difficult for them to refuse our pig plan. I'll make sure they can't do without me."

Stevens flew in a month later.

He opened his briefcase and put a file on the living room table.

"The Bondan Valley has become interesting. What have you heard about a highway from Dagwia directly to the coast?"

"Just rumours," said Ben.

"It's more than that. This is from the Chief Minister's Department."

He pushed the file towards him.

"Read it while I take a look at the stock."

Stevens' brain was humming. A route had been surveyed. A one-in-twelve gradient was possible right through to Poltino Harbour. A profound shift in economic structure was on its way. Towns like Dagwia, and stations like Ongwa, would soon be infinitely more important than they were now.

He looked at the bungalow. And then the paddocks where the failed plantation's coffee bushes had been grubbed out.

"Your idea was a good one, but your timing was dreadful," he told the original owner. "For coffee, cattle – and pigs – the sky's the limit now."

"Ben," he said. "You're the right man, in the right place, at the right time. The road's a national priority. The government's throwing everything at it. It may be completed more quickly than the surveyor's report suggests. Let's examine our options."

These included the development of a pig farm if the Lutherenes gave permission.

Stevens had decided that Ben was an asset Macarunda could not lose.

And if a pig farm meant Hilda and her family would be happier, and him more settled, then so be it.

He followed her into a crowded ward where many patients were bandaged and some had disfigured limbs. Others had pink, pigment-free, splashes on their faces, arms or legs.

"These are our lepers. The pink areas show where open sores have been healed. Some patients still need regular injections, then tendon surgery and physiotherapy so they can recover full use of their hands or feet," she said.

One group was helping each other to straighten fingers or stretch stiff ankles and wrists.

Hilda moved to another giving themselves injections. She spoke in their local language.

"Put the needle in more slowly. Release the medicine slowly too."

He could see a man with no lips, no eyes, and no nose.

"Yaws," said Hilda, "He's from the back of Kwishebe. We can't treat him. He came in too late."

The first trucks from Poltino began to dribble in a year later. They carried rolled steel building frames, ton after ton of cement, disassembled coffee driers, welding equipment, more heifers for Ongwa, others for the Department of Agriculture, second-hand tractors, new trailers, and tray after tray of young coffee bushes.

The dribble became a flood when the road widened and infrastructure improved. They carried everything from drums of engine grease and fuel tanks to copper pipes and corrugated iron.

Kunjin's Ongil clan planted more coffee. They were encouraged by the manager of a new coffee drier who had been told he could expand into roasting if he could guarantee a steady bean supply.

Pita Kunjin BSc (Hons) Agriculture arrived too. His accent was Australian, he dressed Australian, and his family were in awe.

"I'm here to stay," he said.

Hilda sat with him for hours.

"He will do it if he likes the set up," she said.

Ben sat down with Pita as well.

"It's all about arithmetic," he said. "We can produce a 200-dollar pig in less than four months if we feed six-week old weaners ad-lib concentrate with a protein content of 14-16 per cent. I've checked the landing cost, road freight cost, and Lutherene Mission rent. If we can sell at one dollar a live pound, half of that will be profit which we divide among ourselves. That calculation includes a deduction of twenty-two dollars for the weaned piglet. It does not include wages."

Pita's eyebrows lifted.

"One hundred dollars a pig. One hundred per cent profit?"

"Oh yes," said Ben. "For as long as the people in this valley continue to kill huge numbers at traditional feasts, have the money to pay for them, and costs stay the same."

"We will always enjoy eating pig," said Pita. "Coffee is generating new income too. How do we breed the piglets?"

"We'll start with local stock. I'll buy them," said Ben.

"How do we formalise this arrangement?"

"I'll draw up a contract to be signed by myself, Hilda, yourself and your father. Pastor Schmidt will witness it and then we'll shake hands."

They filed into Schmidt's office.

The contract was signed. Hands were shaken.

Ben and Pita signed a lease agreement with Schmidt as well.

They called their business Hilbenkunpit.

That night Hilda told him she wanted a baby.

"Signing that paper was like being married. You are not going to leave me now."

Kunjin told Ben the Ongil elders wanted to see him.

A man with thin legs, and ragged shorts, was waiting for him. He gestured conspiratorially towards a hut doorway.

Hilda was there to translate.

"This is Kamtai," she said. "He has something to show you."

Ben ducked his head and followed Kamtai inside. Other Ongil elders shuffled after him. They lined up in front of a large homemade table.

"This is what we ate before you Europeans arrived," said Kamtai.

His face creased into a conjurer's smile.

"We scoured the bush so you could see for yourself."

Ben moved closer to the neat display.

Kamtai was earnest as he pointed to each banana leaf platter in turn.

"You'll recognise these witchetty grubs. These are baby mice. When we were children, it was our job to find the nests and dig them out. We hunted for all kinds of birds' eggs. We robbed nests of their fledglings. Even little ones like these. Spiders' eggs have surprisingly big yolks. We ate ants' eggs too."

He snorted at the memory.

"Today we can buy tinned fish and bully beef anytime we want to. But when we were children we had to live like our fathers and sometimes we had almost nothing."

The old men laughed.

"Look at these earth worms," said Kamtai. "Four kinds but the red ones were best. Frogs. Tadpoles. Caterpillars. Maggots like these. Sometimes little fish."

He flung out both arms.

"We ate almost everything. If it moved and if we could catch it, we mixed it with sweet potato or taro, then we ate it."

Another old man interrupted.

"It wasn't always so bad. Sometimes a hunter came back with a big bird or possum," he said. "On special days, really special days like weddings and funerals, our fathers would kill pigs. Just as we do now."

Kamtai reasserted himself.

"But they weren't enough on their own. We were pot bellied back then because we did not have enough of the right kind of food. It was only after we could buy meat and fish from trade stores that our stomachs flattened. We look at our children. Like Pita. Like Hilda. Their skin shines. They have muscle. They eat meat every day. They don't get sick as often we did. Their bones are white, their blood is red, and their brains are grey."

The District Administrator had asked Macarunda to walk twenty new heifers to a station in central Kwishebe. Ben took Kobe and four men. They were returning after making the delivery when a man wearing a helmet of cassowary feathers stepped onto the track.

He had blackened his face with soot, was carrying a spear, and a cassowary's shin bone had been pushed through a hole in the septum of his nose.

"He say trouble next village," explained Kobe. "Two man die."

Nose Bone spoke again. He was emphatic.

"He say not good thing we go."

"We go," said Ben.

Kobe and Nose Bone had a long discussion.

"He show safe way," said Kobe.

The headman was relieved to see them.

They were shown two bodies. The left side of their necks had been slashed open.

"Axe," said the headman. He smacked the side of his own neck twice to emphasise the accuracy of the blows.

"He like man go same time us. Report dead killing Dagwia," said Kobe. "Me think not good thing. Men who do this watch road. If see him they kill him."

"Who go with us?" said Ben.

Kobe pointed to Nose Bone who looked unhappy.

"Tell him I got shotgun," said Ben. "It look after him."

He stuffed the left hand pocket of his bush shirt with cartridges.

Three days later Nose Bone sat down in the District Administrator's office.

He had found six good gilts but Pita was unhappy with their boar.

"Too old fashioned. Too much shoulder. Too much snout. Not big enough in the rear end. Too much hair. On top of that there's a colour problem. Our people prefer pigs with black skins and will pay more for them. Some like pigs with ginger skins. Pigs with random spots, whatever the colour, are run of the mill.

"And we need to reinforce hybrid vigour. To really mix the genes. Have bigger litters and heavier weaning weights. I think the Bondan people will like what we produce. We should expect them to buy mainly male pigs to kill at feasts and take most of our females for breeding.

Ben thought modern, pure-bred, Large Black and Tamworth boars should be their target. Pastor Schmidt identified Lutherene Missions on the coast that stocked them. Ben visited his bank, Pita took off in the Landcruiser to collect them and Hilbenkunpit built a farrowing unit next to the finishing pens.

A letter telling him Kit had died arrived the same week Hilda told him she was pregnant.

"What was your grandfather's name?" she said. "What kind of man was he?"

Ben told her Kit and Meg had five children, he looked after his family, worked hard on his farm and tobacco smoke had stained his white moustache.

Hilda patted her belly.

"If this child is male his name will be Kit and your grandfather will have a replacement."

CHAPTER FOURTEEN

Change-change

Kunjin sat with Hilda and Ben.

Her hibiscus were a bank of pink blossom and both bamboo clumps whispered. Stevens' avocado tree prospered against a sunny wall and the hills on the far side of the Bondan river stood clear.

"We have got boundary worries," he said.

Hilda translated.

"The Kisip clan face the same problems as us. They have more children, use more land to grow food, and are clearing more bush for new businesses like cattle or coffee. We used to think there was enough for everybody. But now they are claiming ground we say belongs to us."

She turned to Ben.

"This is serious. In the old days we would kill people who tried to take our land."

"Have you told the District Administrator?"

"He was not much help," said Kunjin. "We said one thing. The Kisip said another. Then they said something and we said they were wrong. His head became dizzy. He said we must find a solution ourselves."

Ben sat down with Pita.

"I should talk to the Kisip," he said. "They know I'm not Ongil. It'll be easier for them to listen to me than it would be to listen to you."

"What would you say?"

"I'd ask them to show me their cattle and coffee. See if I can find ways of helping them increase output and earn more money without making trouble."

"You should take Bakam from your work line with you. He's Kisip."

The Kisip headman was Gabua.

He agreed it would be a good idea to pay someone from the Department of Agriculture to prune their coffee bushes.

"And show you how to do it as well," prompted Ben.

Their cattle were a bigger problem. Once again the challenge was in-breeding.

"You have to change your big bull now," he said.

Gabua shook his head.

"He still young fella."

"You like father marry daughter?"

Gabua shook his head emphatically.

"It same with cow," said Ben. "Not good thing if father daughter make baby."

"Your line hear my talk? Or ear blocked?" he asked Bakam.

"They hear you. Know you frighten bad Kwishebe men. Know you strong. Know you straight. So listen."

Ben swapped the Kisip stock bull for a bull from Ongwa that had served his time.

"You get bigger calf now. In three year change again."

Is your grandmother still alive?" said Hilda.

"I hope so."

"Tell me about her."

He thought for some time. Where should he start? How much would she understand?

"Meg and Kit were a team. Their first thought was family. They both wanted the same thing and helped each other to get it.

"He did heavy work like ploughing, looking after the horses, lambing ewes, digging the vegetable garden and milking cows.

"She turned their milk into more valuable butter and made sure both he, and their children, were clean, well clothed and well fed."

"Did she earn her own money?"

"She kept some that she made selling butter and eggs so she could manage the house. But she saved more by making clothes, preparing and cooking almost all their food, and baking her own bread."

"Did she have a house-girl?"

He laughed.

"My mother and my aunts helped when they were old enough and before they got married. Otherwise, she did everything herself. Washing, ironing, cleaning. Even made carpets. She milked the goat and looked after the pig and hens as well."

"Did she have kitchen machines?"

"Her kitchen had a glass window, solid doors and good furniture but in other ways it was exactly like a village house except it was made of stone. No electricity. No piped water. Just a fireplace which heated her oven and warmed the room. She lit a Tilly Lamp at night."

Hilda shook her head.

"What about your mother?

"We had electricity and running water. Hot and cold. She still worked hard but her life was easier. Just like it is for us."

The first Hilbenkunpit bacon weight pigs were sold for their asking price. No one quibbled. Some buyers wanted to take weaners too.

Word spread. Village people came to see how fast they could grow for themselves.

"It's their feed," said Pita.

"It's magic," was the reply.

"So far so good," said Ben.

Hilda's bamboos were wonderful. They caught the gentlest breeze and were never still.

Sometimes they sighed, more often they rustled, and when they frothed their hollow tubes beat like drums.

Her hands were across her belly.

"It's a boy," she said. "I can tell."

He had been resting his eyes on the hills and the river.

"How do you feel?" he said.

She reached over and put a hand on his thigh.

"Excited."

Alice loved flowering pot plants. She displayed them wherever she could.

When he was in his mid-teens he had stooped to examine her most recent triumph – an unusual, suspended trumpet.

It had reminded him of a Foxglove except it was much bigger.

He had investigated its depths, the intricacy of its design, the complexity of its colours.

It had conquered his senses. He was completely overcome.

The interior of the flower briefly became his existence.

Its beauty had mastered him.

Taken him down an endless tunnel.

He had stepped back in shock.

He was appalled to have been so profoundly distracted.

And had told himself he would not be diverted by anything so abstract again.

He felt the same now. Hilda's serenity, the whispering bamboo, the unusual clarity of the mountain air, and the timelessness of the valley, threatened to overwhelm him.

He shook his head to clear it.

She was alert to his moods and smiled.

Her face shone more brightly than any flower.

Catherine stepped down from her lorry.

A man in riding breeches approached. She'd sold to him before.

"Do you want to check him out?"

Breeches nodded and began to lower the doors.

The gelding was a sixteen-hand chestnut with an even blaze.

"Kybo's a handsome lad," Catherine said.

She led him to an arena and began to lunge him.

Kybo walked, trotted, cantered and turned, on command.

Breeches watched carefully then signalled he'd seen enough.

He patted Kybo's neck then ran the palm of his hand down each of his front legs.

"Habit," he said apologetically. "Know he's been vetted. Cash or cheque?"

"Cash is always welcome," said Catherine. "You can mix it if you wish."

They left Kybo and retreated to his kitchen where he counted out two hundred pounds in fivers and wrote a cheque for four.

Catherine handed ten pounds back.

"For luck."

Hilda began her labour at four in the morning.

She shook him awake.

"He's coming," she said as she dressed.

He drove her to the Lutherene Mission and held her arm as they walked to the delivery unit.

Hannes, the Austrian gynaecologist, smiled reassuringly when Ben kissed Hilda and left.

Kunjin and Pita joined him on the veranda just as the sun struggled over the horizon.

"I'll see how she's getting on," he said.

He immediately knew something was wrong.

People were rushing round but no one would look at him.

There was blood on Hannes' sleeve when he came through the unit's double doors.

"Your son is very well. But Hilda is haemorrhaging. We're doing our best but so far we've been unable to stop it."

"Can I see her?" said Ben.

"Not yet," said Hannes. "Sister Margaret will show you her baby."

Margaret was troubled when she handed his son over.

Kit's face was crumpled. His body was slack. He looked like he'd been in a fight.

"It was a struggle, wasn't it?"

She nodded.

"He's perfectly healthy. Unfortunately, Hilda is not."

"Is she conscious?"

Margaret nodded again.

He handed Kit back.

"Then I'm going in."

He had to scrub his hands and put on a gown but was eventually able to stroke her face.

She opened her eyes and smiled.

He thought his heart would burst.

A blood transfusion unit hovered above her.

Yet another bottle was changed.

"You have to leave," said Hannes.

When he kissed Hilda, her eyes could only flutter.

He sat down with Kunjin and Pita.

The older man already knew.

"Something no good come up?" he said.

"Hilda not good. Man baby good," said Ben.

Kunjin nodded grimly.

Pita held his head in his hands.

She died an hour later.

"Hilda go. Kit come," said Kunjin. "Change-change. Always same."

She had been buried at Komun. In its tam-tam beside untold generations of family that had gone before.

Pastor Schmidt had conducted a service. When he'd left the Ongil had sat at her grave in silence for the rest of the day.

Their son would not be short of love, thought Ben.

Kit was being kissed and cuddled as he was passed around the circle of relatives sitting on the floor of Kunjin's hut.

Pita had taken him after they came back from the hospital.

"We'll look after him. He'll be safe with us."

Ben, numb to his core, had let him go then opened the door to his desolately empty house.

He could not look after a newborn baby. The Ongil could.

"Do what thing now?" asked Kunjin.

Ben mumbled something incoherent and watched Kit being suckled by a young Komun mother.

The child was sleeping contentedly when he held him too.

He organised a truck to take Ongwa's surplus bulling heifers to a new home, arranged repairs to the loading ramp, checked the boundary fence, and settled into his paperwork.

A letter from the UK, impossible to miss in its distinctive airmail envelope, had arrived.

It was from Meg. She would like to see him, just for a short time, while she was still strong.

He knew that if he did go home he would not come back.

He discussed this with Pita who knew that without Hilda's care Ben would soon be a driverless car.

"You need to be with your people," he said. "Just seeing them will make you feel better."

Ben thought about this when he was in bed, when he was working, and when he sat under Hilda's bamboos. He decided Pita was right.

He called on Pastor Schmidt.

"We need to re-organise Hilbenkunpit."

They agreed the venture would prosper and could soon need a bigger building.

Then Schmidt took notes.

The Lutherene Mission would abandon the lease and become a partner. Ben's share of the profits would be placed in a trust fund for Kit until he became a full partner when he was twenty one.

Kunjin, Pita and the Lutherenes would share the rest. The Lutherene cut would be forty percent.

But if audited profit topped a pre-agreed sum then each partner would transfer one per cent of their dividend to Ben through a nominated UK bank account at the end of each financial year.

Schmidt and Pita would act as trustees for Kit until he was twenty one.

Pita supported this and persuaded Kunjin to as well.

A new Hilbenkunpit agreement was signed.

And Ben set up an external account in Morwick to transfer his Pagamban assets.

These would include his savings and a termination payment from Macarunda.

He told Pita to re-invest the bulk of Hilbenkunpit's profit in buildings and breeding stock then make sure the Kisip continued to prune their coffee bushes and changed their bull every three years. There was nothing left to do so he kissed Kit and flew home.

Alice didn't recognise him when he walked in.

It wasn't the tan. Wasn't because he was seven years older. It was because he'd lost so much weight. He was stick thin.

She could see the sadness on him.

"I'll get your old room ready."

He walked over to see Meg. Each was shocked when they saw the other. She was stick thin too.

She boiled tea. Put out sandwiches and cake.

"Eat up".

"Catherine's buying and selling more horses than anyone this side of Timbuktu. No sign of a husband. Spoiled for choice that girl."

"Tom's the clever one. Going to be a doctor. We need someone to look after us."

CHAPTER FIFTEEN

Belinda

"What are you doing?"

It was Judy Clark. She was standing with two little girls and he was at Whiteside's annual show.

He had a camera in one hand and was flapping a catalogue with the other.

Jim Henderson was in front of them. He was holding a Black and White third calver with a red rosette tied to her halter.

"My cousin's cow won her class. He wants her picture in the paper. She'd look her best if both ears were pointing forward."

He gave her the catalogue.

"Stand next to me. Give it a shake when I tell you to."

Judy shook, the cow's ears pricked, the shutter of Ben's camera clicked and Jim said "that's good."

He turned towards her.

"How are you?"

"Can I pat her?" said the eldest girl.

"No worries," he said and led them to her stall.

He stood next to them while they stroked her shoulder.

"What's she called?" asked the youngest.

"Belinda. I knew her grandmother."

She wasn't sure if he was being funny or serious.

"Let's get some ice cream," he said to Judy. "I'll take a picture of the girls holding cones and patting Belinda at the same time."

"You've got an Australian accent," she said as they stood in the queue.

"What would you say if I offered the picture to the Morwick Gazette?" he replied.

He'd decided to shoot off a roll and test the editor's reaction.

He positioned Judy and the girls around an obliging Belinda, snapped off a quartet of shots, and took out a pen.

"I need your names for the caption."

"I'm Julie," said the eldest.

"Harriet," said her sister, hiding her head.

"And your surname?"

"Johnston," said Judy.

"Where do you live?"

"Crown Lane."

"What a surprise," said Ben to himself.

He took pictures of Colonel Leighton handing a cup to Ted Hogarth who'd won the "Best Kept Frontage" competition, then Geordie Elliott who'd taken most points for flower arrangement, Mary Dodd for baking, Malcom Thompson for Supreme Sheep and Raymond Laidlaw for Best Show Cow.

"Didn't recognise you, Ben, you jolly tinker," said Geordie, shaking his hand. "Haven't seen you for ages."

The Gazette editor accepted his film and captions.

His photos were published that Friday.

Judy, Belinda, and the girls were on the front page.

Alice took two phone calls. The first was from the Gazette.

"Where did you learn to take good pictures?" said the Editor when Ben rang back.

The second was from Judy asking if he'd like to come over on Sunday afternoon.

Judy's home, Crown House, was huge. So was her lawn.

He was pleased they were outside. It made conversation easier.

Julie, and Harriet – "My real name's Hattie" – hovered shyly by his chair.

"How did you know Belinda's grandmother?" said Hattie, looking at her feet.

"She was always last out of the field when I called the cows she was with in for milking. I'd walk beside her with my hand on her back."

He made them laugh with stories about other animals on Bill Henderson's farm then they wandered off to play on a swing.

"Where's Mr Johnston?" he asked, expecting to be told he was earning pots of money overseas.

"Charles died two years ago," said Judy. "What about you?"

"Never had time to get married," said Ben.

He was offered a job at the Gazette and took it.

He was employed not just for his photography but because he was familiar with farming.

"We don't know the difference between a hogget and a heifer," said the News Editor.

Most of his articles were presented straight down the middle but if an opportunity for slant was offered, he almost always backed the underdog.

Local knowledge was an asset, so was his ability to take pictures covering his own stories, and so were the Gazette's archives.

Their range of miscellany was endless. He had not known a scar beside Glenton Beck had been used as a Black Death burial pit and records confirmed a landslip in the 1700s had exposed a "sepulchre of bones".

And he enjoyed tilting his lance at the pompous.

Habits acquired at Discipulum still lingered and would die hard.

"Another by-line and another front page photo," said Judy. "You're taking over."

"Fluke," said Ben. "Would you help me look for a house?"

His Pagamban money had arrived and it was burning a hole in his bank account. Inflation was almost twenty-five per cent and if they were not invested in property, his savings would melt.

He had something like £20,000 in hand and could take out a mortgage calculated at two and a half times his meagre Gazette salary at an interest charge of only nine per cent. This arithmetic underlined a profound contradiction. It made sense to buy at the top of his range using as much borrowed money as he could pull together.

"What kind?" she said.

"Something with a shed and a front field. I want to keep a horse."

He moved into a four roomed cottage at the end of its own lane. It had a two-acre paddock and an outbuilding that could be used as a stable and store tools. It needed a damp proof course, new windows, a new kitchen, central heating, and a shower. Jim re-seeded the paddock and worked with him to concrete the yard.

He asked Judy if she'd help him buy curtains, carpets, and furniture.

"What if I'm too bossy?" she replied.

After he moved into Fine Cottage he hung clusters of framed A4 photos on the walls.

Some showed his family, some were from Discipulum, there was one of him riding Matey at Walrooba, and a handful from Pagamba.

Stevens was smiling next to him beside a Land Cruiser and Pastor Schmidt had taken a picture of Kunjin, himself, Hilda and Pita just after the contract had been signed. She was holding his left arm with both hands and had rested her head on his shoulder. It was labelled "Hilbenkunpit".

Judy did not walk past it.

"Who is she, Ben?"

She tried to decipher Hilbenkunpit.

"I can see a "Ben". Who are "Hil", "Kun" and "Pit?"

"Hilda, Kunjin and Pita."

"She loves you. She can't hide it. What happened?"

"She died."

"That's why you came back?"

She kissed his lips.

"You've always been easy to like. Let's help each other."

Curtains of Sticky Jack and ramparts of nettles threatened to choke the hedges that surrounded his paddock. He borrowed a knapsack sprayer and Paraquat weedkiller from Jim.

"Be careful with that stuff. Take these gloves and facemask, wear your wellies, and keep the nozzle down," he was told before he took it away.

He felt uneasy using a chemical with a skull and crossbones on its label and a warning "Poison. Do not swallow".

After he'd doused his hedge bottoms he washed out the sprayer, hosed down his wellies, put his shirt and jeans in the laundry basket, and was unusually careful when he cleaned his face, arms and hands.

He collapsed in the shower while he was rinsing his hair.

The spasm that seized his left side began with a knot just above his hip bone and a tentacled spread which threw him to the floor with his left arm in claw position and his right foot kicking a hole in the bathroom door as he tried to relieve the pain.

Doctors were baffled.

"Have you been in contact with any hazardous chemicals?" they asked.

He told them about Paraquat and the DDT that anti-malarial staff in Pagamba had sprayed with abandon both indoors and out.

Some of the government rest huts he'd used while walking cattle on bush trails had been sluiced so often their walls were powdered white.

The exclamation "you've been in the tropics!?", and an accompanying shrug, had been a collective response.

"You could have picked up anything," he was told.

A lumbar puncture was ordered and a doctor sweated nervously as he tried to tap his spinal cord.

"You've a back like a miner," he complained before his needle was eventually manoeuvred through.

"Your sample was cloudy," said the specialist. "You almost certainly have MS."

He was prescribed Carbamazepine and told to take four 100mg tablets a day.

He was ambushed by similar spasms for almost three years. They came without warning, sometimes forcing him to the ground, but their intensity gradually faded.

"Don't use this again!" he had said when he returned the Paraquat.

Jim hid it in the back corner of his chemical store.

"It'll be there 'til Doomsday. What else can I do with it? Can't put it down the drain."

"Can we go to see Belinda?" said Hattie.

"She'll be in her working clothes," said Ben. "Not as clean as she was last time you saw her."

Both girls laughed.

"Better wear wellies," he told Judy. "There'll be muck everywhere."

They timed their arrival at Sunny Banks for afternoon milking. Just before Jim brought in the cows.

They walked down the lane to Rough Strothers and stood by the gate.

"Huff-werff, hufff-werfff. C'mon. Huff-werff".

The herd began to file past. Everyone one of them Black and White. Each with a full udder.

"Can you see her?"

The girls shook their heads.

"Here she is."

Belinda was last to come through.

They walked behind her as she made her way to the byre.

"This is where your milk comes from," he said.

"I haven't seen this before," said Judy.

"Ben has. He's a veteran," said Jim.

He gestured at three teat clusters.

"Stick those on, will you?"

Each cow's name and ration was chalked on a miniature blackboard above her stall.

He gave Fantasy her cake and hoped she'd behave while he fitted the cluster.

He knelt down, muttered "steady girl", and plugged her in.

"See this," he said, pointing to the milk frothing through.

Three heads nodded.

"Stand back," said Ben.

Freckles, the cow in the next stall, had adjusted her hind legs and begun to arch her back.

Torrents of ammoniac urine poured from her gaping vagina. Some splashes hit their feet.

"Good God," said Judy.

Her daughters laughed.

They watched him plug in Heidi, then Gwen, and followed him into the dairy where he opened the tank.

He took a pint measure and filled it.

"Have a sip."

Hattie asked why it was warm.

"Would you like to visit my grandmother?"

"Yes, we would," said Judy.

Meg was sitting in front of her cottage.

"Who's this you've brought with you?"

She led them inside.

"Grandma's good at baking," said Ben.

The plates she put in front of them proved it.

"She wore clogs when I was your age," he told the girls.

"I've still got them. They're at the bottom of the scullery cupboard. Right hand side."

He carried them in.

She pointed out their wooden soles and metal trim.

"Try walking in them," she told Judy.

He mock whispered "it's Cinderella" as he helped her put them on.

Editor called him in.

"Captain Thomasin's not happy with our story on his plans to fell Throup Wood. He couldn't complain about its accuracy. It's our angle that's upset him."

Throup Wood was a silhouette of oak that lined a long mound near Whiteside.

His article, and Editor's headline, had suggested a landmark so visually pleasant should not be removed.

The Parish Council chairman and a local haulier had agreed.

"There'll be a letter from him this Friday. He can't do anything else. I like these non-diary pieces. Dig out more if you can."

It had been a strong letter.

But the reaction was not what Thomasin expected.

Two replies dominated discussion the following week. One was from another landowner. The other from a neighbouring parish council. And each agreed that prominent deciduous features like Throup Wood should not be demolished.

"Why so much fuss about some trees?" asked Judy.

He took her to Whiteside.

"We're going to walk to Wheelstones."

Syke Wood beckoned. It was months since he'd last been through.

Rabbits were feeding, there were more deer, a first badger sett, and the beech cathedral was magnificent.

"If we come back in October it'll be even better."

After he closed the last wicket gate, he stared at Wheelstones for a long time.

"What is it?" asked Judy.

He shook his head.

"We have a farmer who ploughs right up to his field edge and another who always leaves a verge," said Editor. "They both think they're right and they've been arguing with each other at farm meetings for months. Now it's gone public. Our letters page is already showing reaction. Can you put together something that fuels the fire?"

Douglas Storey was desperate. Harold Toward was trying to play a long game.

"These are my fields and I want to get as much off them as I can," said Storey.

"High yields are essential. My farm couldn't be profitable without them," said Toward. "But I won't take out hedges to make my fields bigger and crop every inch of ground as well."

"Hedges are a nuisance, ponds get in the way and wildlife doesn't help me recover my costs," said Storey.

"Insects that live in field edges help to pollinate my crops. And the farm would be a lonely place if there were fewer birds," countered Toward.

"I must slap on the nitrogen. It's the only way I can beat low market prices," Storey insisted.

"I try to look after my soil. Cow muck, crop rotation, trace elements, phosphate and potash. Test it for deficiencies every five years. Dress with slag or lime if necessary," said Toward.

"I'm going to drill more wheat and use more nitrogen to get the yields I need," said Storey.

"That'll exhaust the soil. Make it difficult to grow decent crops if the markets come good," said Toward.

"What do you think?" said Editor.

"High costs and low grain prices are a perennial problem, but Storey is extreme."

The Gazette's letters page buzzed for weeks.

Most correspondents were in favour of hedges, ponds and wildlife. They also wanted cheap food.

"Gunner will be the best hunter in Morvale," said Catherine.

The eighteen-hand gelding was roan with four socks.

"He's Irish. Showjumper sire and Clydesdale dam. I'd say he was a one-off. Jump anything and carry you all day."

"How'd you find him?"

"Tip off. Last owner went bust."

"He's five years old and came with his tack. You can have him for £900, I'll winter him but if you don't take him home and get him fit he'll be wasted."

He part-exchanged his van for a second-hand Land Rover, bought a half-decent Ifor Williams trailer, and took Gunner to Fine Cottage. The gelding was so long he had to stand diagonally to fit in.

He learned a lot about Irish hunting on his new horse.

The Morvale's approach was disciplined.

Field Master's word was law. He led a crocodile of followers over his chosen course and his field formed polite queues at the first run of jumps.

He knew the country. The best routes, safest crossings, the most difficult obstacles, and exactly where they could and could not go.

The Irish packs Gunner had hunted with must have allowed riders to take their own line. He charged every obstruction and frothed if he was forced to wait his turn.

He was not wicked. Just unfamiliar with restraint. And so strong, such an athlete, that if he hit second stride he could not be stopped.

"What a horse," said Field Master. "Where did you find him?"

"Through Catherine. Where do you think?" said Mrs Golightly.

She circled him on her new bay.

"Best example of his type I've seen."

Gunner rode on.

"Sorry," said Ben as the roan, impatient at having to wait in an orderly line, picked his own, more difficult spot and jumped it instead.

"Sorry," he said as Gunner, partnered by a universal intake of breath, strode over yet another high tensile fence.

And "sorry" yet again when he hurdled a gate instead of the milder obstacle beside it.

It was easier later in the day when the field had either thinned down or was strung out.

But for the first hour it was always a battle between Gunner's enthusiasm and Morvale control.

He hoped Field Master was right and he'd settle down.

A bored American millionaire had decided he wanted to shoot grouse and bought a wide moor behind Whiteside. He'd also decided he didn't want sheep on it. Some flocks had grazed there for generations. If access was blocked there would be nowhere else to put them.

One farmer had rung Ben to complain. But when he turned out to meet them not all the new owner's tenants were friendly.

"If you annoy him, it'll make him even more awkward."

They were tough men. They could walk the moors in all weathers. But they lived off land that had been owned by someone else since feudal times, understood the weight of a landowner's whim, and were anxious.

"He's got it wrong about sheep," said their host. "If they came off, the heather would soon be waist high and there'd be nothing for him to shoot. What are his 'keepers telling him? They know grouse like young heather. They'll go somewhere else if they're hungry."

"And beaters couldn't walk through it," said another.

"What about burning?" said Ben.

"He'd have to do it more often. It would be difficult to control. Don't think he'd ever get on top of it. But what's the point of trying when sheep can do his work for him?"

No one dared mention hefting. That if their flocks were taken off open moor for more than a short time they could never go back on because replacement females, the ewe lambs, would not have been trained by their mothers to recognise the invisible boundaries between each farm's grazing allotment. It was a result too dismal to contemplate.

The survival of an established sheep husbandry system, and the wellbeing of the community that surrounded it, hinged on persuading a financial whizz-kid that tradition had virtues too.

CHAPTER SIXTEEN

Parturition is brutal and bloody

He opened his front door and could see nothing but snow. Not a rolling sweep of unspoiled perfection but a blank wall embedded with flawless imprints of his doorknob and letter box. The same drift had smothered the west side of the house and filled his yard. He was buried in and until snow blowers had pushed through his daily routine was suspended.

He rang his Discipulum contacts. Farid was working for Magnum, Chris was on a Sunday broadsheet, Maggie did features for the BBC and Daryl freelanced from Westminster.

They joked about him living in the back of beyond.

When he protested they laughed. "Why are you wasting your time up there" was the common theme. "This is where the action is."

He thought about their response each time he stepped outside to check the weather. The sky was unbroken blue, the landscape without blemish, and he had not heard silence so profound since he'd moved through mountain passes in Pagamba.

He began to dig out his yard, stopping mid-shovel, to listen to nothing – not even sheep. He scattered some horse feed. Hungry Yellow Hammers and noisy House Sparrows were first to flock in.

He wanted to be successful, feel satisfied with his work, without having to endure the nightmare of living in London.

So little was understood about food production. It was rarely taken seriously. But he'd seen undernourished people in Pagamba's deep bush, pot-bellied children watching him listlessly from the shadow of their huts and the profound impact of a wider diet on their health, energy, and strength.

No one in Morwick made soup from sheep's heads any longer. WW2's food shortages were already being forgotten. Politicians took supplies for granted. People hurrying through their now weekly shop did too.

The world re-claimed him slowly. Billy Turnbull from nearby Bamchester was first to arrive. He was trying to cover sections of his milk round on foot. Bulldozers and snow blowers began to be heard. Their near primordial growling still distant. The following afternoon an exhausted postman fronted up and the machines crept closer.

On the third day Tommy Tyson came in cross-country with a bucket on his front end loader to clear his lane and a snowblower rumbled past his road end that evening. Traffic began to trail after it. He would drive to Morwick next morning. The stillness was over.

Noise picked up immediately. Meg was taken to hospital with pneumonia. She died, the last of her generation, less than a week later and was buried, with Kit, in the Anglican church yard at St John's. He stood with Scott, Alice, Catherine, and Tom in puddled snow at their graveside. Judy was at his shoulder. The Sunny Banks Hendersons had lined up opposite. Other aunts, uncles and cousins completed a circle in which almost everyone carried a durable, self-reliant, understated stamp. Some older men had been made crooked by relentless physical work. Many women had arthritic hands. The Kerrs stood close by.

Generations of his family had been buried there. Generations to come would be too. The churchyard was notoriously wet and there were stories of coffins bobbing in their grave even as earth was being thrown on top of them. Meg's Aunt Catherine had been lowered into a puddle. He'd been told many times that poor Katy could not swim. He waited his turn to throw in a spadeful of earth and winced as it rattled against already half covered wood. Her clogs were buried with her.

They crossed the road to the Parish Hall where life immediately took over. Trestle tables carried more food than people could eat and teacups never stood empty. Edward Kerr was talking to Judy. Alice and her sisters had made a noisy triangle. Catherine had linked arms with Alf. He and Tom put their heads together. His brother expected to qualify that summer and hoped to become a surgeon.

"Ben," she said. "We should live together."
    She was right.

"We could convert the downstairs granny flat into an office. If people wanted to see you they could use the side door. We could sleep in the front bedroom."

That was sensible. They'd used it before.

"And we could get married."

She was right about that too.

"Hilda had a son."

She did not look surprised.

"He's called Kit."

"Where is he now?"

"With his Grandfather Kunjin, and Uncle Pita at Komun."

"How do you know that?"

"I trust them."

"What about his education?"

"Pita has an honours degree from Brisbane University and Hilda was a qualified staff nurse. The Lutherene Mission smoothed their way. It'll do the same for Kit if he wants it to."

"He could come here."

Ben shook his head.

"He'll be running round barefoot in the same raggedy shorts as other Ongil kids. If he came to live here it would break him."

"Have you written to him?"

"He wouldn't know me from Adam, but I am in touch with Pita."

"Have you sent him any money?"

"Before I left I made sure he would be looked after."

Mrs Thatcher was using interest rates to hammer down inflation and mortgage charges had soared to seventeen per cent.

Charles had done his best for Judy but repayments hovering on £200 a month had not been in his plans.

Ben had to help out and at the same time keep Fine Cottage afloat.

Regular income from Hilbenkunpit was still some way off.

The venture was thriving. Pigs in the Bondan Valley had become even more valuable because more coffee was being grown. But weaners were easily stolen and the unit had to be protected by an expensive security fence.

"The price of success," Pita had written. "Weaners are too tempting. The worst thieves were truck drivers who tucked them under their arm then did a runner."

Polaroid photos showed the hen shed had been converted to house more breeding sows and the finishing unit had been extended.

He had married Matrissia Waia and Kit lived with them. The boy would soon be taking lessons at the Lutherene Mission School. Pastor Schmidt hoped Ben was well and passed on his best wishes.

"Buy me a pint," said Gethryn Jones.

He was the Ministry of Agriculture's regional livestock specialist, and it was Friday lunchtime in Morwick.

"What do you know about EU plans for a new sheep support system?"

He produced a foolscap sheet which listed fifty-two end of week dates followed by a figure.

"This," he said as his forefinger stabbed the final column, "will be the guaranteed value of every fat lamb sold in the UK that week".

"Actual market price will be deducted and vendors paid the difference."

The make-up payments would be huge.

"We have to thank the French," said Gethryn. "Their lamb sells for much more than ours – which is why the guarantee is so high."

"For lowly Brits who give their lamb away for next to nothing it's a bonanza."

Ben wanted to know when the information would become public.

"Not for another month."

"Can I keep this?"

"Why d'you think I gave it to you?"

He offered the story to Farming Times.

It was sceptical.

"How did you get this? We've not heard from you before. We'll publish four paragraphs on an inside page. We daren't do more."

The Ministry rushed to confirm the schedule, and other payment details, the following week.

"We got that wrong," said Farming Times. "Could you do more work for us?"

"I'm pleased I'm pregnant," said Judy.

Morning sun was streaming through their bedroom windows and they could hear the girls chattering in theirs.

He put his hand on her tummy. So was he.

When she'd first told him his head had filled with contrary thoughts.

She put an arm across his chest and kissed him.

"I'm surprised how easy it is to love another man."

Chris rang from London to ask what he knew about disposals by British Nuclear Fuels at Sellafield of radioactive wastewater into the Irish Sea.

"Nothing yet," was his reply.

He rang him back half an hour later.

"They're not doing anything noisy but there's a meeting in a local hotel tonight. Some people have kicked up a fuss and need to be calmed down."

Gosforth was about five miles from Sellafield on the A595.

He had put on a Barbour jacket and when he sat in a back corner he looked no different from farmers who were already there.

He rang Chris from a public call box.

"The discharge is being described as radioactive solvent, volumes may be huge and the Irish are hopping mad."

He gave the names of the people on the platform and a summary of what they had said.

He'd learned much more by being invisible than he would have done if he'd sat scribbling in the front row.

"You'll get a tip-off payment but we can't give you a by-line," said Chris. "I'll make sure the right people know."

He approached his Building Society, asked if he could take out a bigger mortgage on Fine Cottage, then passed over his most recent bank statements and accounts.

The manager tapped out a calculation and agreed that he could.

The original mortgage had been tiny, He was earning more than twice what he had been, and the house had jumped in value so the Society, which was enjoying interest payments at 17.5%, was pleased to double his burden, and he was pleased to take a cheque for almost £8,000.

"We have to talk money."

She nodded.

"Could you sell this place and live somewhere smaller?"

She shook her head.

"Only if I had to. The girls are too settled."

He explained his new Building Society arrangement.

"I'm being, we're being, forced into a corner. If I continue to increase my earnings I could use Fine Cottage as a bank, re-mortage every time a lift in income makes it worthwhile and help you out with your payments.

"But if the Society thinks this is my principal residence, which it would be after we marry, it might not be so accommodating.

"I could rent Fine Cottage to someone who keeps a horse. But if I did that I'd risk losing the opportunity to repeatedly re-mortgage, so if inflation stays where it is we may not be much better off."

"We're still getting married?"

"We are."

"Doesn't that mean that you'd own half the house?"

"Makes no difference. We'd still have to meet its mortgage payments, but I don't earn anywhere near as much as Charles did, and if we didn't we'd lose it."

"What would you do?"

"Get a tenant into Fine Cottage and commit to living here."

"What's the problem?"

"The problem, Judy, is that if I did that, and we didn't drop our standard of living, I'd have to work like a dog. Up to sixteen hours some days. Perhaps six days some weeks. Working freelance. At the beck and call of as many editors, sub-editors, as I can pull together, the deadlines they'd insist on and which I'd have to keep."

He did not tell her income from Hilbenkunpit would begin to trickle in before the end of the year.

She did not say she still wanted to play tennis and golf.

She did think being pregnant was yet another worry.

She tried not to think about who would help to look after Julie and Hattie if he wasn't there.

She did say to herself I love him.

He did say to himself I love her.

He did not say Crown Lane was where snobs lived.

She did not say he was a village boy.

He did think she had a most kissable mouth.

She did think his eyes were like nobody else's.

They married.

Parturition is brutal and bloody. It always had been and always will.

He knew first hand it killed women. It always had and always would.

It killed babies as well. It was a bet against a tragic outcome. A calculated roll of the dice.

"You're doing very well, Mrs Robson," said the boss nurse.

"Fast shallow breaths."

Judy panted dutifully.

He was standing to one side.

Parturition had no dignity either.

She was naked, on her back, knees wide apart, belly huge, everything exposed.

No wonder she was frightened. How could she force an eight-pound baby out?

"Let's have a push," said Boss Nurse.

Judy pushed.

Boss Nurse waited – almost beating time.

"And another."

Judy pushed again.

"That's enough. Catch your breath."

Judy panted.

Her head turned towards him.

He moved next to her and held her hand.

"Push!!" said Boss Nurse.

"Push!!!"

Judy pushed, pushed and pushed. Gave up and lay back panting.

He'd seen Boss Nurse roll her eyes.

"One last big one," he whispered. "You almost did it."

Her grip on his hand tightened.

Boss Nurse waited. The palm of her hand on Judy's tummy – listening to silent time.

"Now," she ordered. "Now. One last effort."

"Push."

"Push!"

"Push!!"

Judy pushed and groaned.

Pushed and groaned.

And pusssshhhheddd and groanedddd again.

"Good girl," said Ben.

Boss Nurse reached forward with busy hands, gave her bloody bundle a fierce, professional once-over, then smiled.

"He's a healthy boy."

Judy laughed.

The baby suspended in Boss Nurse's grip had a petulant lip and a scrotum that hung like a sack.

"I can see that," she said before kissing him when he was put on her chest.

"Parturition is wonderful too," he said to himself.

He was once again surprised the baby he was holding felt boneless. Almost rubbery. Without form.

Judy, completely naked, surprisingly normal without her belly, watched while a nurse washed blood off her legs.

He handed him back and she held him to a breast.

She'd done it before.

"Come on, little man," she said as she cradled him and kissed the top of his head.

"First suck."

CHAPTER SEVENTEEN

Special advisor

"I need someone with overview," said Gethryn Jones. "Not looking for a technician. I want perspective."

"To do what?"

"Work for me. On the side. Go to meetings if I ask you to. Be my ears. On most occasions you'd be able to write what you like, for as many people as you like, afterwards, but I'd want to hear from you first."

Ben was silent.

"I could offer a retainer. I'd not call on you often but when I did I'd want you to earn it."

"You'd be tipping me off if something interesting's happening as long I gave you a ring before I start writing?"

"That's about it. I'm surrounded by people who do their best to understand Westminster, and the European Commission, but need someone who's had muck on his hands and got a grasp of what's happening on the ground."

Ben liked Gethryn. They had often joked about the gap between practical farming and central administration. The difference between a boot and a suit. But he'd been promoted to Director of Livestock at the Ministry, sat in a private office in Whitehall, and that made him a suit.

"You meet regularly with the farmers' organisations," he said.

"They're group thinkers. Their core interest is membership. Retention first. Expansion if possible. They've undoubted influence but they're reluctant to be positive on issues that might rock their revenue boat. And can shout too loudly, and about the wrong thing, if their membership demands it. They're not always objective."

"You want me to spy for you?"

"No. I want to hear what you think."

There was a long silence.

"What would your retainer be?"

Gethryn named a sum.

"I'd put you down as a special advisor and that's exactly how you should think of yourself."

"OK," said Ben.

"And it's strictly confidential. You must not tell anyone. Not even your wife."

Ben agreed.

"You can start now. A father and son partnership in Sussex is being harassed by an awkward landlord. You can turn yourself into a crusader. Make as much noise as you like. I only want publicity."

Gethryn gave him their names, address, and phone number.

He was a crusader too.

The farm was old fashioned. Traditional buildings, a midden in front of the byres, and a hayshed instead of a silage pit.

They sat in their kitchen with Ben. The men wore bib and brace overalls and their wellies stood beside the back door.

"He just walks in," said Mr Peakman. "First time he went straight upstairs, opened every door, and started taking notes."

"I was making the beds," said Mrs Peakman. "Asked him what he was doing. Got no answer."

"He did the same outside," said Mr Peakman. "Poked his nose into everything, didn't say a word, not a peep, then drove off."

Their bachelor son sat with his chin on his chest, saying nothing.

The old man started to cry.

"When he came back the second time he had an assistant who helped him measure every room. We've lived here all our lives. He told us we were going to be evicted."

"A new landlord, son of the old one, wants to cash in on the rural housing boom and is trying to bully his tenants off," he told Gethryn.

"The old man's past sixty-five and the landlord's saying he'll go to a tribunal to prove the son's incompetent."

"Is he?"

"No. He's not ambitious but his stock management's good and their grass management is better than average. They've a low input, low output system. No big buildings. No big machines. No overdraft. Just an old-fashioned family with modest drawings content to live within their means. I haven't seen their accounts but I'm told they show a positive balance. Dilapidations next to nothing. They look like easy meat."

"What have you done?"

"Taken their photo. They look like they're at a wake. Got shots of some good cows, decent pasture and new fencing. Farming Times will run a story. South of England regionals will too."

"Have they got a solicitor?"

"Never entered their heads."

"Tell them to ring this one."

The garden at Crown House was south facing, almost all lawn, with a huge copper beech and several oak on steeper ground to the rear. Each spring a cloud of bluebells appeared beneath them.

Julie was leaning back on a rope swing, trailing her hair, watching blue tits hunt out caterpillars, and the shifting leaf patterns above her.

Hattie sat cross-legged with her sketch pad.

Aaron wobbled past on his balancer burdened Striker.

Abel gurgled while he played with his toes in a pram.

"Somone's missing," Judy had said one mealtime.

"There's a space that needs to be filled."

That night they played Snakes and Ladders. Judy liked family games. She wanted the children to do things together.

"It's about life," said Ben when Julie complained she was too old.

Aaron just enjoyed it. He whooped when his counter climbed a ladder and groaned when it slid down a snake.

"Why's it like life?" asked Julie.

"It's full of ups and down," said Judy.

"Just like this board. Full of nothing else," said Ben.

Julie looked at him and then at her mother.

She thought she understood what they meant.

"A West Country dairy farmer had an abortion storm three years ago," said Gethryn.

"He got on top of the problem but his bank is making him sell in-calf heifers to pay his overdraft's interest."

Ben shook his head. A dairy farm had to sell milk. Produce as much as possible. If it lost its in-calf heifers it would earn progressively less without reducing its fixed costs and would eventually go out of business.

"It's hard to believe."

"That's what I said. But it's correct nonetheless."

The Pringles had planned to milk 150 cows but were down to eighty-five and their herd, like their income, was still shrinking.

They showed him twenty replacement heifers.

"We wanted to calve these at two years old to put quick milk in the tank. They're almost due," said the father.

"We've been told to sell them next week," said the son.

Ben shook his head.

"Come inside and we'll show you."

"Their account is with a local branch. The manager is a keen young man who's out of his depth," he told Gethryn.

"They were in intermittent debt four years ago, always before harvest, but their overdraft is currently £260,000 and rising."

"What have you done?"

"Nothing yet."

"I'll ring you tomorrow."

"It underlines a national problem," said Gethryn.

"Agricultural management, particularly arable, pigs and dairying, is deeply technical and must be cost responsive, but some local managers still think it's rustic."

"More specialists, men who deal with nothing but agriculture, and know how farms should be run, are being appointed but the process is far from complete."

"I want to hurry it up."

"Make as much noise as you can."

It looked like it might be too late for the Pringles.

"Do you know a Malcom Osborne Seagram Musgrove?" Ben was asked over the phone.

He did. Musgrove was senior accountant in a Bristol firm that specialised in receivership.

"He's coming here on Friday morning. What should we do?" asked Mrs Pringle

"Call your solicitor. I'll come along too."

It was a typical farm living room. A square table with six chairs, an oilcloth cover and a fruit bowl. A sideboard, a friendly fire, an old sofa and battered easy chairs lined its walls.

"Would you like to sit at the table?" Mrs Pringle asked Musgrove when he came in with his briefcase. "A cup of tea? A biscuit?"

He sat down. Pringle and his sons sat opposite. Ben was in an easy chair. So was the Pringles' solicitor.

"There you go," she said as she put down his cup. "The biscuits are on the sideboard. Which ones would you like?"

Musgrove turned to look. A plate of Ginger Snaps and another of Custard Creams sat in front of a 12-bore shotgun.

He looked back at the Pringles. Then their fruit bowl which brimmed with No 6 cartridges.

"Let me introduce you to everyone," said Pringle.

"Mr Thompson is from Lloyd, Garnier and Preston. He's here to persuade you our overdraft is the bank's fault and should be written off."

"Mr Robson writes for several newspapers and wants to know why our overdraft has become as big as it is."

"These are our sons. Teddy and Fred. Teddy was going to shoot pigeons this morning but stayed behind when he heard you were coming."

"He doesn't want to sell any more heifers and he wants to inherit the farm."

Musgrove was waiting next to his car.

"Did you put them up to that?"

Ben shook his head.

"It wasn't James Thompson either. He's still telling them off."

"Were they serious?"

"What do you think?"

He rang the bank's national agriculture manager the following morning.

"Hello Henry. I'm looking at a £280,000 farm overdraft. Would it be possible to ask you some questions?"

He heard National Manager spring to attention.

"Have you an account number? Can you confirm the branch?"

Ben read them out.

"I'll ring you back," said National Manager as he slammed down the phone.

"You've more neck than a bull," said Gethryn.

Ben had faxed him a copy of the Pringles' most recent bank statement.

It confirmed a £320,000 overdraft had been written off.

Farming Times had negotiated an exclusive.

A follow up statement by the Pringles had been faxed to radio and TV as well.

He thought building a drystone wall was like writing an article. The same progressive construction then a solid, satisfying result. The founds were the opening paragraph, courses were the theme, jumpers were explosive adjectives, and throughs were verbs. It could be argued, he said to himself, that fillers, the fragments that were packed into gaps, wedged wobblers and reinforced stability, were punctuation and well-shaped face stones were nouns. Might a link stone, a narrow insertion that made sure an awkward joint had been crossed, be an adverb? But what then was a cope or a quoin?

He'd put in a terrace at Crown House, to break a slope, raided abandoned field boundaries in Forestry

Commission plantations for throughs to make a bog garden, and now he was working on a pond. Not an ordinary pond. It would be ringed by a flagged path, a low semi-circle of stone would make a south-facing seat, and a patio on its west side would be shielded by a seven foot wall. It would be a work of art. He loathed messy cement. It was just as effective to build a wall with natural joints that leaned in on itself to be solid.

Edward Kerr tipped another trailer load of stone.

"There's plenty more."

Judy joined them.

"Dad always said he was a natural," he told her. "If he hadn't gone to college he could have put up walls for a living instead."

"I need flags and quoins," said Ben as they drank coffee.

"Brocksburn's taken down an old byre. It had a stone roof," Edward replied.

He took a sip.

"Not long 'til cubbing, Ben. Will we be seeing more of you then?"

He spooned in sugar.

"Catherine's got a new boyfriend as well as a fresh horse."

"When's she getting married?" said Judy.

"Who knows?"

"When's Floss having another litter?" said Ben.

"Not for a while. Looking for a pup?"

"Put me down for a bitch."

"Is Floss a collie?" asked Judy at lunchtime.

"You've seen her. She's their yard dog. Not a worker. Happy to hang around the steading. Barks when people walk in then tries to lick their hands."

"Why a bitch?"

"Less likely to wander off. Dogs go raking."

"I'll tell the children at dinner time."

"No, you won't. Floss isn't in pup yet."

"Is there a problem?"

"I want them to be ready for her first. Collies are good dogs. Really loyal but they're active as well. If we did have one we'd have to look after her properly. Walk her twice a day. For at least half an hour. Most of it off the lead. We'd need to take turns. And she'd have to be trained. Come the second she's called and stop whatever she's doing the moment she's asked."

Gethryn named a supermarket. One of the top six.

Then its red meat buyer, Neil Hull.

"They're all hardnosed but he's special."

He wanted Ben to challenge him – if he could find a finisher, or a slaughterer, who'd speak out.

"He's cheating on payment weight. I don't know how. Perhaps you'll be able to tell me?"

The conference venue was London. The theme was boosting beef sales.

The Minister of Agriculture was saying British beef was the best in the world. The processors flanking him paid farmers who supplied them with cattle some of the lowest prices in the EU but still nodded like dogs.

Hull sat with them. A powerful man with a Welsh accent, a shock of blond hair, and a hard face.

When he made his presentation, he immediately claimed his company retailed more beef than any other in the UK and that made him Britain's biggest cattle buyer.

Ben could have named at least two that were even bigger but when the Minister nodded in acceptance Hull struggled to hide his smirk.

"Glad I don't have to work for him," whispered Cathy Ferguson.

She staffed for The Scottish Post.

He stood up at question time.

"Could the panel describe company spec and explain its function?"

Hull's head shot up. The processors caught the Chairman's eye and quietly shook their heads.

"Perhaps Neil can answer that?" Chairman said.

"Don't know what he's talking about," Hull replied.

Chairman was about to move on to the next question when a man in a striped suit lifted his hand.

"Jens Kaalund. European Commission."

"Company specification is illegal. Cattle carcases must be trimmed precisely to the template framed by one of four official dressing specifications and purchase price per carcase kilo should be adjusted to their pre-determined level of trim. Our New EC specification is favoured by the majority of supermarket suppliers because its trim is the most severe."

Kaalund lifted his voice.

"That means it allows the stripping of most fat. To compensate for the reduced weight the price per kilo should be adjusted upwards. A supermarket supplier can trim back as far as his retail customer demands after a carcase has been weighed for payment. And most do."

Kaalund paused.

"However, our understanding is that some processors are weighing carcases for payment when more brisket and topside fat than there should have been, as well as large sections of neck and flank, has been removed before the carcase reaches the scales. This creates problems for farmers at two levels. They will be unable to compare inter-abattoir payments accurately because offending plants will not have restrained their trimming to the same official, pre-determined, level.

"And an abattoir that trims heavily may offer a price in pence per carcase kilo terms that appears favourable because it stands above its competitors but is not enough to compensate for tissue that should have been paid for but did not reach the scale.

"In other words, many farmers are being short changed because the calculation that fixes their payment is not being made against a common, legally agreed, official template.

"I'm not pointing a finger at any company here. Or naming names. But I am saying the Commission takes a dim view of excessive trimming, will investigate malpractice, and will take punitive action if necessary."

Ben put his hand up.

"Does the introduction of company specification mean farmers who would like to compare the carcase offer presented by a range of abattoirs can't do so accurately because it's impossible for them to match like with like?"

"Yes," said Kaalund.

"Can it also mean an attractive, high pence per kilo, offer made by fieldsmen working for an abattoir that uses company specification is almost certainly misleading because payment on a whole carcase basis will be lower?"

"Yes."

"Can you confirm, for simplicity's sake, that if an abattoir dresses to its own company specification its suppliers are almost certainly being cheated?"

"Yes."

"What was that about?" asked Cathy.

"Tell you later," said Ben.

He studied the Minister, then the other speakers, and turned to look at the room.

The Minister was disinterested. The other speakers were annoyed. The conference delegates were confused.

Kaalund approached him.

"What do you know?"

"At least two of Hull's suppliers write "company" in the specification tick box on farmers' kill sheets."

"Could you fax me some examples?"

"Meat Inspectors must be collaborating," Ben said.

"Some must be," Kaalund agreed. "Company specification is illegal. I need to have a word with the Minister's accompanying official."

Ben suggested he got in touch with Gethryn instead.

Hull stood directly in front of him.

He was furious.

"I should cut your tongue out," he said.

He meant it.

He was surrounded when he got back to the Press Room.

"What was that about?" they said.

He repeated what Kaalund had said.

Few were wiser.

"If it's too technical for you lot what chance have farmers got?"

"I've got it," said Joe Wallen.

He leaned forward and whispered.

"You've got it," Ben replied.

"I haven't," said Cathy.

Several others mumbled "neither have I".

"It's simple," said Ben. "Farmers trading cattle with some of the companies that supply Hull's supermarket think they are being paid more even though they're being paid less."

Catherine had at last got married. Julie and Hattie were bridesmaids and Aaron was a solemn page boy.

Her husband's surname was Beltingham-Norris-d'Antille.

"His family's covered a lot of options," said Edward. "The mother must have been a friendly girl."

"She'll be made for life," said Alf.

Ben knew better.

"You almost hooked a Duke," he'd teased.

"Wait till you see the house."

Livinton Hall, an unadorned, one-time fortress, stood foursquare at the head of its valley.

Crispin's mother had met them at the front door.

"Really pleased to meet you, Benjamin. I'm Hortense. Don't trip over these."

"These" were buckets spread haphazardly over her reception hall's hardwood floor.

"Roof's a mess. It rained last night."

She opened a door. Shut it. Tried another and shut it too.

"Let's use the kitchen. At least it will be warm."

Crispin's father had been called in.

"I'm Jonathon. Welcome to our decaying domicile," he'd said as he shook Ben's hand.

"Cris and his father won't abandon the house," she'd said on the journey back. "They really won't. The family's lived there since dot. They've no cash but they won't give in. Re-leading the roof's the priority. Its £8 a foot and they'll need to install miles of it. Cris wants to open the grounds as a visitor attraction to raise money and thinks horse trekking would be a lure."

He was amazed how quickly Judy's new pond had stocked itself.

Frogspawn and toadspawn had appeared overnight.

She'd added water lilies and iris. He'd put in pond weed. And the children had insisted on goldfish.

Newts, caddis, snails and water boatmen, arriving from nowhere, moved in soon after.

He sat watching it now. It was endlessly restful.

Newts were his favourite. They skulked under lily pads, or drifted with fronds of pond weed, like miniature dinosaurs.

There were two types. Julie, Hattie and Aaron had been sworn to secrecy. No one had ever seen Greater Crested. Weren't they abnormally rare?

Water boatmen were busy things. Caddis were brutes. Dragon Flies, iridescent green and blue, either whizzed past or hovered.

Herons flapped in to feed.

And there were slow worms in the wall.

His word processor and printer made writing easier and his fax droned constantly as pre-ordered copy was despatched to a long list of destinations, including Brussels.

Nevertheless, his work pace was cruel, his telephone demanding, deadlines inflexible and travel was a chore.

He would, if he had been able to snatch the time, have watched the pond for hours.

"There will be rules," said Judy.

"Floss's pup can have a bed in here during the day."

She pointed to a corner next to the kitchen table.

"But at night she'll sleep next to the side porch radiator, and she must never, I mean never, go past here."

She opened, then shut, the door between the kitchen and the rest of the house.

"Those are my conditions. Am I clear?"

Floss's pups lay with her, on straw, in the corner of a redundant byre.

All of them black and white and all keen for distraction.

"There's three bitches," said Edward.

He picked them out. Julie, Hattie and Aaron knelt to stroke them.

"Take your time," said Ben. "They'll all be different."

Two were brighter than the other.

The pup with a white head, and a single diagonal splotch over an ear and an eye, had struggled into Julie's lap and was licking her hand.

"I like this one," she said.

"So do I," said Hattie.

Aaron decided he did too.

"I'm not betting on a name," said Edward.

"Hasn't she got one?" said Hattie.

"She's wearing it," said Ben.

"Patch!" said Julie, clapping her hands.

Patch had cried for her mother all night.

She'd also shat next to her basket.

"We have to do this to stop her," he said as he pushed her nose in it.

"Ugghhh," said Hattie.

"I want her to think the same."

He buried her nose again repeating "No. No. No".

"Take her outside and make a fuss of her when she widdles."

He took a call from Gethryn mid-morning.

"Sorry to bother you over a Bank Holiday. Have you been keeping up with the news?"

He had.

"The radioactive drift from Chernobyl that moved over the UK last night ran into heavy rain over the West Pennines, South-West Scotland, and Wales. There will have been fallout in those areas."

"Cabinet's principal concern at this stage is misinformation spread and the avoidance of panic. My current focus is on the possibility that fallout will contaminate grazing livestock."

"Not humans?"

"Only if they eat nothing but grass. I want to hear or read everything you can give me. Notes summarising local TV and radio broadcasts. Fax me cuttings of what you think's interesting and phone immediately if you pick up noisy reaction. Nothing I've said is to be repeated."

He took calls from several news editors looking for on the ground updates.

Also from journalists keen to find out what he knew and discuss whether the information they'd picked up was solid.

He summarised his observations for Gethryn then typed up what he could for his customers.

He was at a livestock conference in Scotland when a Ministry of Agriculture official publicly linked caesium-137 contamination levels with locations that had caught most rain.

There is a silence that confirms unusual audience attentiveness. He could hear people listening.

"Hills and mountains are worst affected. Lowland contamination is negligible."

"Concentrations are heaviest on hill farms in Dumfries and Galloway, the Southern Lake District and North Wales."

"That means sheep farms," said Joe Wallen.

"That's correct."

Gethryn confirmed this.

"There was short-term panic in Westminster. Ten thousand hill farms could face movement and sales restrictions because radiation levels within their flocks are too high. But there's profound relief most of the drift blew over."

He was walking through Fullers Burn, to skim stones in the Morton with Hattie and Patch, when he saw Cissie Lish.

"Now then, Ben. How'yer keepin?"

He told her.

"Where yer at?"

"Up the hill."

She nodded.

"Thowt yer wad be."

"What about you?"

"Ah'm senior checker at t' garment factory."

She puffed her chest.

"Married wi' two bairns an all."

She tilted her chin towards Hattie.

"She one o' yours?"

"One of four, Cissie."

"Yer've been a busy lad."

She tickled Patch's ears.

"Got a bonny dog an' a bonny dowter an arl."

"What's your husband's name."

"Jack. Jack Hall. Foreman at t' foundry. Wah got a hoose up on Glebelands. Three bedrooms. Ah'm doon here tae see me Mam."

"You'll be Town Mayor next."

She laughed.

"No chance o' that. Nice seein' yer, Ben. Ah've got to be off."

"Goodbye Mrs Hall," said Hattie.

Cissie lifted her hand as she left.

It was the garden that pleased him most. No one could overlook them and he had only to walk a hundred yards to reach a footpath that led to fields.

Their children, and their friends, liked it too. An old shed had become a den, he could improvise a plastic water slide on hot afternoons and there was a miniature billiard table, and an old sofa, in what had been a garage.

Judy could entertain hers beside the pond, or on a patio in front of the side porch, and he'd rented a nearby paddock where he could summer Gunner then get him fit for cubbing.

When he was at home he took Patch there twice a day and in evenings tried to take one of the children too. They always kept a close eye on new badger sett and a den where vixens reared cubs. One evening Hattie had spotted an owlet, on an overhanging branch, a mallard and her brood in military formation as they hurried through a pool, and a water vole sitting on a flat stone cleaning its whiskers.

He still joked about having to persuade Julie not to take every orchid she saw home for her mother, and ever-present red squirrels entertained them all.

In winter he watched them through his office windows as they hurried, tails flicking, along their interlinked tree branch roads. They hopped across the lawns in summer and bustled inside a long hazel hedge each autumn.

Every bush shook and shivered.

"It's alive," said Aaron.

"How many are in there," asked Abel.

CHAPTER EIGHTEEN

Mad Cow Disease

M rs Thatcher's free market philosophy had a long arm.

She'd been out of office for five years but her fondness for deregulation still had wheels and the Milk Marketing Board was about to be dismantled.

It had been established during the 1930s depression to stop farmers being ripped off by manipulative dairies and put a bottom under their milk sales by being the buyer of last resort.

That meant allowing milk processors to have their pick of available supplies then sweeping up everything they turned their backs on at a pre-agreed floor price.

Kit had sworn by the MMB.

"Times were hard when it wasn't there. The dairies would send milk back if they didn't want it. Sometimes it was already sour. We could only give it to the pig. That's why Meg started to make her own butter."

Henderson was uneasy.

"I wouldn't trust them an inch," he said. "You watch. They'll promise the earth while they're recruiting then drop the price as soon as they get things stitched."

Jim was more optimistic. A dairy in Manningham was offering much more than the MMB for the grade of milk produced by Sunny Banks and he wanted to sign a contract.

Ben's thoughts mirrored his uncle's. He thought Jim would soon be disappointed because a general fall in farm milk prices was inevitable the moment dairies secured control.

Edward Kerr was more worried about floundering cows.

"There was another on TV."

"The one who can't get onto her front legs when she's trying to stand up?" said Ben.

Edward nodded.

"What's BSE?"

"A spongy brain."

"What's the cause?"

"No one knows."

Aaron and Abel preferred rowing to horses.

He blamed their High School PE master, a Dutchman who'd been an Oxford Blue, and was fanatic.

It owned a boat house on the Morton and each Saturday the boys joined scores of children who submitted to bossy coxes and heaved their craft up and down the river.

Aaron was already going to regattas. Sometimes getting up at 5am with a long drive ahead of him before as little as twenty minutes on the water then another long drive back.

He and his crew improved. They still endured early starts and late finishes but occasionally won their class, raced a second time, and sometimes came home with miniature medals.

Ben bought an Ergometer. It stood in the old garage and whirred each evening.

He watched them at home regattas in summer but could not get excited.

In winter he took Gunner hunting and left rowing to Judy.

PE Master told him they were team players.

Their Ergometer began to whirr more loudly and more often.

"The Ministry's banned meat and bone meal," said Farming Times. "Just got the press release. What do you know?"

He rang Gethryn.

"Our scientists have constructed a theory. BSE's being re-cycled."

"In what way?"

"Infected brains within meat and bone meal."

"How many might there have been?"

"Could have been thousands."

"How many cases have been confirmed?"

"Perhaps four thousand over the last twelve months."

"Four thousand?"

"And rising."

There was a long pause.

"I'll give you two telephone numbers," said Gethryn, "if you promise not to let me down."

"Why do you need reassurance?"

"Because BSE in Britain could become an international news story and the politics surrounding it are already sensitive."

One of the new contacts was a senior epidemiologist. The other a senior vet.

"I must spell things out," said Gethryn. "Nothing they might say will ever be attributable. Just background for you to build on.

"And they too will have to trust you. I'll make sure they know who you are but if you let them down they won't take a call from you again."

It was a relief to clear his head while out hunting.

He and Gunner were one of Field Master's self-appointed ducklings.

There were six of them, they knew each other's riding style, trusted each other's horses, and like ducklings formed a line immediately behind him and followed wherever he chose to go.

"Where's he taking us?" said Becky Bamford.

"He's betting Charlie turned towards Hangmans Hill after he crossed the beck," said Don Taylor.

"That'd be right," said Ben as Gunner prepared himself for the next jump.

He'd been told more times than he could count he rode an exceptional horse.

Catherine had confirmed it when she'd last taken him out.

"Amazing for his age. Never put a foot wrong."

The hounds were out of hearing but there was no stopping Gunner.

He knew exactly where he was and where he had to go.

He took a hurdle without breaking stride and settled into a long canter to Dolly Wood.

Ben looked behind him. The ducklings had spread into a wide vee.

Becky smiled. Paul Pescott lifted a hand.

Professor Richard Lacey had triggered national alarm.

BSE had already been transmitted to thousands of humans, he'd claimed.

The illness would be progressively debilitating, and death would be slow.

Perhaps half a million people could be struck down over the next fifteen years. Emergency hospitals would have to be built but there might not be enough nurses to staff them because they too would be among the infected and unable to look after themselves.

In the meantime, all six million of the UK's cattle would have to be slaughtered and their carcases destroyed.

The media clamour was overwhelming.

"Is there anything you feel able to tell me," Ben asked Epidemiologist.

"The effectiveness or otherwise of our 1988 ban on the feeding of meat and bone meal is critical. BSE has a four-to-five year incubation period so it will be at least two years before we begin to find out."

"Is there anything else you think I should know?"

"Confirmed cases in cattle have lifted to fifteen thousand over the past twelve months and could double over the next two years."

In 1996 Parliament was told BSE infected beef was killing people.

A week later the European Commission banned the export of UK product.

Cases had peaked at 36,000 head in 1992 and dropped to 10,000 in 1995.

"Does this mean the meat and bone meal ban is working?" he asked Senior Vet.

"It's encouraging but there could be a sting in its tail."

"Cattle born after the 1988 ban have been infected," said Epidemiologist. "If you wait a week you'll find out why."

A revised rule, from then on known within Whitehall as the Real Ban, was introduced and possession of meat and bone meal was outlawed. Stocks bought before 1988 had been held over on some farms and some had continued to be fed to cattle.

"Hit this as hard as you can. We want every last ounce removed," said Senior Vet.

"We're convinced that only tissue from the nervous system can carry infection," said Epidemiologist.

"But we've lost eight years because the original restrictions were incomplete."

Farmers with cattle became punch drunk.

Every animal older than 30 months that was presented for slaughter had to be destroyed.

The brain, spinal cord, and other tissue with nervous system links, taken from younger cattle was incinerated, and no retail beef could be sold on the bone.

An upside was that surprisingly resilient consumption was reinforced by a lift in beef quality because everything on offer was from young animals and the best cuts were no longer being exported then replaced by beef taken from older, tougher, stock.

A downside was that the biggest processing companies could no longer wave two fingers at price-hungry supermarkets because they were supplying higher paying customers on the Continent and had to submit to penny-pinching contracts designed by the hard-nosed domestic buyers they'd been doing their best to avoid.

Beef cattle continued to be sold for much less than it cost to produce them.

"How much does the Livinton Estate have in hand now?"

He and Catherine were grooming Gunner.

"About 3,000 acres including hill ground and forestry. It's enough. We don't need more."

"How's the pony trekking?"

"Slow. Not as useful as my livery. We need ideas. You should come over."

She stepped back.

"He's showing his age, Ben. Are you up for another?"

"His younger brother?"

She laughed.

"Bring him to Livinton when the season's finished. I'll do my best to dig out a replacement."

"You've got to get onto email," said Cathy. "Watch this."

They were in a press room and she'd finished her report on the meeting they'd just attended.

"The news editor wants 300 words ASAP but I won't be phoning it in."

Her fingers flicked over her word processor's keyboard. She frowned and stabbed a key.

"It's loaded."

She pointed.

"That's the newsroom's email address. Hit the button and it's off."

She pressed "send".

"They've got it. Could already be sub-editing. What were you going to do?"

"Cook it while I'm driving home and fax it out this evening."

"No good, Ben. Not when people like me can jump in first."

She called Joe Wallen over.

"Ben's going to frame his report on the way home and fax it out later."

Joe shook his head.

"You know news editors. They grab what comes first. If Cathy was a bandit she could email her article to all your customers."

He opened a Hotmail account later that week and made his fax machine redundant.

It was the end of an era.

He'd developed a market with a score of regional papers, weeklies and dailies, which were satisfied with the fax deliveries he'd tailored to suit them.

But the freelance market had become even more competitive. Now every journalist with an email account had become a rival able to flash, straight onto a newsroom's screen, as much as they wanted, whenever they wanted, to whoever they wanted, and, as Joe had said, news editors, not always tuned in to informed agricultural reporting, often snatched at whatever arrived first.

"He'll be good," said Catherine as they loaded Captain. He was coal black apart from a thin blaze and three socks.

"Bang up to weight and he's got presence as well. Carried the flag at last year's Hawick Common Ridings so knows how to handle soft ground."

"I'm keeping Gunner. There'll be a queue for him when we start trekking again."

Her father-in-law was determined to fight to the end.

"D'Antilles have lived here since the Conquest," said Jonathon Beltingham-Norris-d'Antille. "And they always will."

"Past grandmothers had to marry into the Norris and Beltingham to maintain the inheritance, but they didn't give up the d'Antille name."

"Cris and Catherine think the same. Jonathon and Julian will too. We won't let it go."

"Is there anything you think I should know?" he asked Epidemiologist.

Papers rustled. He could hear pages being flipped.

"Weekly cases continue to reduce but there's no avoiding the feared long tail."

He confirmed a precise case figure that was encouraging but was gloomy about a quick finish.

"The re-cycling of infected brain tissue through meat and bone meal was the core problem. We're convinced of that. But the Real Ban won't have the same impact as the 1988 ban because the volume of proscribed tissue that continued to be fed over the interim period was extraordinarily low."

"Risk is the trigger word and as long as confirmed cases continue to dribble in, even just one a month, regulators and politicians will continue to be cautious."

Did this mean the Over Thirty Month rule might not be lifted for some time?

When would British beef exports be given the thumbs up?

"All BSE controls will be removed at some stage and British beef will be universally accepted as safe. But failure to anticipate meat and bone meal continuing to be fed, albeit in extremely small quantities, for eight years after the original ban has imposed its own, self-determining, delay."

"Quality beats quantity," said Ben to himself as he emailed his summary of the conversation to his listed news desks.

But exclusives were jam. Routine stories, picked up at press conferences at the same time as other journalists, had been his bread and butter.

He would continue to file specials gleaned from contacts he'd telephoned on a one-to-one basis, but knew competition created by email would make his freelance income shrink.

They were standing in line at the top of Wenside. The night was cold and a blazing comet was powering across the south-west sky.

"We're just a speck," said Ben.

"That's deep," said Hattie.

"Look at it. Where'd it come from. How did it get there?"

"Who's we?" said Aaron.

"Human beings," said Ben. "We think we're the centre of everything."

"When's it coming back?" said Abel.

"Tomorrow night," said Judy.

"I meant the next time?"

"When we're long gone," said Ben.

CHAPTER NINETEEN

Hello Grandmother

"Would you like a freebie?" said Gethryn. "The German Embassy wants to show us how well they're re-modelling former collective farms in the East."

"Selected journalists have been invited to Berlin. You'd be one of three Brits."

They were bussed from their hotel on Unter den Linden to a different farm each morning and always passed scores of abandoned army barracks, row after row of already mouldering grey Nissen huts, on the way.

The common feature of collective farms was their inefficiency. Acreages were huge but stocking rates, like profits, were thin.

"We sometimes think their principal function was not to produce food but to provide work for as many families as possible," said a guide pointing to yet another labour compound surrounded by almost empty fields.

"What was this dairy farm's average lactational yield?" asked Joe Wallen.

"Acceptable. We think something like 5,000 litres."

"How many cows?"

"Six hundred."

"Area?"

"Fifteen hundred hectares."

EC stocking rates were at least twice as high.

"Why so much labour?"

"Only the cowmen could milk. Tractor drivers could only drive tractors. Fencers fence. Ditchers ditch. Welders weld. There was no multi-tasking."

"What were their wages?"

"About 60 per cent lower than those in the West."

"Were there other handicaps?"

"Run down machinery. Outdated buildings. Poor practice. Output measured against each labour unit was less than half West German levels."

When he stepped out from under the frowning Prussian portico of a history museum and looked towards the drab brick structure that had been Erich Honecker's administrative headquarters, an understanding of architecture hit him like a blast.

The museum had been designed to be imperial, militaristic, Teutonic, and intimidating. He could feel Bismark's strength. Honecker's HQ was understated, empty of ambition; it could not risk being imposing. It was a building that had been cowed by Moscow's scowl.

It had not dared square its shoulders or jut its chin. Its sole function was to house filing cabinets, pen pushing clerks, telephones, carbon paper and desks. It, like the now empty barracks, had emphatically been just another of the Soviet bureaucracy's many enforcement tools.

Unter den Linden had been hollow as well. Its lime trees were gentle and frontages modern, but there were bomb sites just thirty yards to the rear, and arcing sprays from machine guns, presumably Russian because they'd been pointing westwards, still scarred derelict buildings.

The Brandenburg Gate was different. Newsreel pictures of Hitler and his Nazi troops filing triumphantly under its eagle topped chariot were as familiar to him as the guard being changed at Buckingham Palace. A German soldier who had marched through may have killed his Robson grandfather at Passchendaele or wounded his father near Tunis. Nevertheless, he had already accepted that new Berlin could eventually be the epicentre of a re-united Europe.

A dog's just killed three of our lambs," said Edward Kerr. "Can you get a photo in the Gazette?"

"Did you see it?"

"Big black thing. Looked like an Alsatian."

"See the owner?"

"No."

It had done more than rip the life out of three lambs.

The rest of the flock was standing, still stressed, in a field corner. Some had bites on their necks, hind legs, and shoulders.

Edward had heaped the dead lambs together.

Ben rearranged them so the spread and depth of their wounds was more obvious, then asked Edward, his anger unmistakeable, to kneel behind them.

"Had you seen the dog before?"

Edward shook his head.

"We're starting to get people walking across the farm," said Henderson. "You know the footpath but they don't use it. Last weekend there were four of them. They didn't have a dog but they went straight through the cows. I had a word with them. Asked them to stick to the path. They told me they'd done nothing wrong. I asked where they were from. One said it's none of my business. Another said they lived in Morwick."

"Did you hear about that woman from Demesne who got trampled?" said Alice. "She went through some suckler cows with her dog on a lead."

"What happened?" asked Ben.

"She picked it up when they came after it. They knocked her down to get at it. Trod all over her."

"Did they have calves?"

Alice nodded.

"What happened to the dog?"

"It ran off."

Ben remembered standing with Farid in 1967 when students had, almost overnight, begun to wear long hair or short skirts and carry placards.

"Something's happening," he'd said. "Can't you smell it?"

That had been a revolution. A sudden, near simultaneous, shift in attitude.

Was something similar happening again?

Was public access to wide rural spaces becoming more important than the production of food?

Were well-fed British people becoming so complacent about predictable supplies they'd forgotten where it came from or how difficult it was to deliver?

Just after he'd been born, sixty per cent of household income was spent on food eaten at home. Ten years later it had dropped to thirty-three per cent. Now it was just eight per cent. Holidays and new cars were much more important. So were the entertainment and status pleasures of dining out.

There was a knock on her front door.

Alice reeled in shock when she opened it.

"Hello Grandmother. I'm Kit."

"I know who you are."

Her hands were on his chest.

She pulled her head back.

His face was still Ben's.

"He came out of nowhere. Like you. Just walked in. Looked just like you. Except thinner. Spoke like an Australian as well."

She eased away.

"Kit was my father's name."

She saw him nod, heard him say "I know", and shook herself.

"Come in. Your Grandad's round the back. I'll ring your dad."

She continued to marvel as they sat opposite each other.

How could two people be so alike?

Kit's skin was browner, and his black hair had more spring, but his eyes were the same deep green and their faces were carbon copies.

He'd picked up a history degree at Brisbane University and had been to Oxford to complete his PhD.

"I'll get Catherine over."

"Judy's on her way," said Ben.

"How's Kunjin?" said Ben when the Robsons had gathered.

"Grandfather died last month," said Kit. "He's buried in the tam-tam at the same place as my mother."

Ben's face was heavy. His British family sat back.

"And Pita?"

"My uncle's very well. He's the Ongil headman now."

Ben asked about Kobe.

"A rascal like he always has been."

Gabua was still the Kisip headman.

"We have a bull changing ceremony every three years."

Hilbenkunpit was flourishing. Ben knew this through Pita's letters, and the regular payments into his bank account, but it was reassuring to have it confirmed first hand.

"Pastor Schmidt's still active. We had to improve the perimeter fence again. The Bondan Valley grows a lot of coffee. There's insatiable demand for pigs."

"What are your plans?

"I'm going home now I've handed in my thesis. Not sure what will happen after that."

Kit stayed with his grandparents for two nights then took a room at Crown House.

Aaron and Abel were overawed.

Patch licked his hand.

"What were you studying for your thesis?" said Ben.

"The many faces of colonialism."

"You must see Livinton Hall."

They ate in the Beltingham-Norris-d'Antille kitchen.

"It would be impossible to conclude a study of the British ruling class without an encounter with a raggy toff," said Jonathon.

"We used to rule India, half the world indeed, but now we find it impossible to keep warm in our homes unless we cower next to an Aga."

Hortense poured more tea.

"Let me show Kit the library," said Jonathon.

Catherine and Cris swapped money-making ideas with Ben.

"You should ask Kit about Hilbenkunpit when he comes back."

He was carrying a book when he did.

"A gift from Jonathon. It's not in the Bodleian. It's a first edition as well."

"Tell us about Hilbenkunpit," said Hortense.

"Wish people had pig feasts round here," said Jonathon when Kit had finished. "It was a brainwave, Ben. Look forward to you coming up with another."

"Where's Great-Grandfather?"

They were in the graveyard at St John's.

Ben pointed. Judy, Hattie and the two boys followed them over.

Kit read the inscription.

"Why's he called Christopher?"

"It's the big name for Kit."

"What was he like?"

"Kind."

"Margaret was my great-grandmother?"

"Meg," said Ben.

"Your Robson Great-Grandfather is buried in Belgium."

"First World War?"

"He was conscripted. Been over there just six weeks."

"Who else is here?"

"Lots of Robsons. Lots of Hendersons."

"Show me."

"I only know where some are buried. Poor people couldn't afford gravestones. Their plots weren't marked. Hendersons had more money than Robsons so you'll see more of theirs."

They toured the graveyard. Aaron and Abel were just as interested as Kit.

"This is my great-uncle, William Robson. He died when I was in Pagamba. He had a Military Medal from the First World War."

"Fighting Germans?"

Ben nodded.

"This is where Kit's parents are buried. They farmed Wheelstones as well."

"This gravestone's interesting. Hannah Robson was born in 1810. She married a rich farmer. That's how we know where she is. Her husband's surname was Skelton. They're still at Low Grange."

He smiled at his sons.

"Your very distant cousins. If we went back far enough you'd find you shared some blood with just about everyone buried here.

"This is a Robson gravestone. The earliest I could find. They farmed twenty-three acres and ran an ale house. Must have earned enough to afford this."

His hand tapped an ornate five feet slab that was smothered with inscriptions.

"John was born in 1764," said Kit.

"How old is this tam-tam?"

"The church was built 300 years ago so it's at least that."

They returned to Kit and Meg.

Ben turned to leave.

"Can you wait for me in the car," said Kit. "I need to think."

"Grandfather, did you fight Germans?"

Scott nodded.

"Ben says you were wounded."

"He was," said Alice. "Bullet through the chest."

"My other grandfather, Kunjin, was a warrior. He fought the Kisip many times and was hit by arrows here, here, and here."

Kit smacked his left shoulder, upper arm, and thigh.

"Where was your wound?"

Scott pointed to the right side of this chest.

"Can you show me?"

He looked at Alice who nodded, stood up, pulled off his shirt, stood for a moment, then turned.

The scars were still angry. Entry was neat. Exit a crater.

Kit muttered something in Bondan. He was shocked.

"What's Livinton's history?" said Ben.

He, Catherine, Cris and Kit were drinking beer.

"Anyone been beheaded? Anything nasty happen in the cellars?"

"Father's the historian," said Cris. "Knows exactly who's lived there and when."

"Not talking about establishment worthies. You need rogues. Traitors. Back-stabbers. Thieves. You need brawls, dungeons and blood. Old blood. Lots of it. The more the better."

He turned to Catherine.

"You need two trekking routes. One long, high and difficult. The other for beginners or just for fun. You need woodland walks. Some interesting animals. Texas Longhorns? Something exotic. Anything. Sabretooth Tigers. Piranhas being fed raw steak."

He paused.

"And when that's assembled you have a big opening day."

"Need an attraction for that," said Cris.

"We could stage a dance," said Kit.

"We?" said Catherine.

"The Ongils. Girls in traditional dress. Men hoisting spears and pretending to fight."

"Journalists would love it," said Ben. "Wild men of Pagamba flock to Livinton to help their poverty-struck British relatives hang on to their stately home."

"It could be done," he said a week later.

Judy, Kit, Hattie, Aaron, Abel, Catherine and Cris were sitting with him.

"Listen to Kit."

"We ask for volunteers in Komun. Unmarried men and women. They come here with their weapons, drums and decoration. Stay in the Hall and dance every day until they go home."

"What do you say, Cris?"

"It's right up Father's street. He'd love it. We're not short of space."

"They'd have to be looked after," said Kit.

"That would not be a problem."

"I could organise press coverage," said Ben. "Imagine Kit in traditional dress leading a pony trek on Gunner. The girls, in shorts and T-shirts with feathers in their hair, greeting people when they come to look through the house."

He scanned the table.

"I'll have to go to Pagamba with Kit. He'll need help kicking this off."

That was true but he would have insisted on a visit even if it was not.

Young people were taller, children were maturing earlier, everyone was better nourished. Roads were wider. Some were tarmacked. Saloon cars mixed with articulated lorries and crowded buses.

Pita's house at Komun had a veranda, rainwater tanks and a corrugated iron roof.

A long wheel base Mitsubishi Shogun utility was parked beside it.

"My wife Matrissia," he said.

They shook hands.

"Our children," he said, pointing to a line of teenagers.

They stared at him wide-eyed. He stared back. He could see traces of Hilda.

They embraced him. The eldest boy was called Kunjin.

Ongil men and women crowded in, some stood on the veranda's steps, others leaned over its rails.

He shook hands with them all.

When he leaned back in his chair he could smell village. Woodsmoke, thatch, bush tobacco and the woven split cane floor. Bamboos were rustling, a cockerel crowed and a baby squawled. The sky was blue and the hills across the Bondan stood clear.

There was a brief commotion when Kobe bustled in.

He grabbed Ben's shoulders.

"We go look Ongil cow?"

They did but he went with Kit and Pita to the tam-tam first.

Pastor Schmidt was pleased to see him.

"You haven't changed a bit."

Schmidt had. He was getting old.

"We should talk about Hilbenkunpit while you are here," he said.

"Its constitution must be re-drafted. Only two of the original founders are still with us, I'm approaching retirement, and new blood is coming through. The Lutherene Mission looks forward to continuing the lease. Our share of its profits has helped to fund a new school and a new hospital ward. Does Kit have a role? Pita may wish to invite Gabua, or another leading Kisip, to take a place on a new board of management?"

Schmidt paused. He fixed his eyes on Pita.

"It may even wish to extend its remit. Offer assistance with education? Sponsor scholarships? Identify specific improvements to local infrastructure? Use its funds to pursue a wider, social development led approach? Think about it. We'll sit down again before Ben goes."

Pita nodded.

"I got that. But first let's hear something from Kit then take Ben to see the pigs."

The original buildings had gone. The new farrowing house had pens for twenty-four sows. Some were suckling litters. He counted fifteen piglets in one. The boars were meaty.

"We import replacements from Australia," said Pita.

The finishing pigs had been sleeping. They woofed and honked as they leaped to their feet then ambled to their trough to chomp more food.

"The biggest market is still traditional. Weddings and feasts."

The fence surrounding the compound was high. Its gate equally imposing.

"Reminds me of Berlin," said Ben.

"Couldn't do without it," said Schmidt. "Helps keep the peace. We haven't lost any stock for three years."

Lunch was relaxed. There was disbelief when Kit described Livinton's leaking roof.

"They're your aunt's in-laws?" asked Schmidt.

"Catherine's children are Kit's cousins," said Ben.

"What would accommodation be like?"

"There's no shortage of rooms."

"I'd suggest a party of no more than twelve young men and twelve young women, and the ideal sleeping arrangement would be dormitories."

"They should be accompanied by a man and a woman of their parents' age. They'd be guardians, cooks, father, mother, run arounds and always on hand."

"If they were in a dormitory together they could chatter and swap notes. If they were on their own they'd have no-one to share their thoughts with and might get depressed. When do you propose to set off?"

"When everything's ready," said Kit.

"Why don't you ask the Pagamban High Commission in London if it could help? If necessary the Lutherene Mission could chip in as well."

CHAPTER TWENTY

Mediaeval funeral pyres

"Foot and Mouth Disease. Officially confirmed. Not on a farm. In pigs at an abattoir in Kent," Joe Waller told fellow journalists as he pocketed his phone.

An FMD epidemic could be apocalyptic. Ben remembered not being allowed to visit Wheelstones and Sunny Banks during an outbreak in his early teens.

"You won't be welcome," Scott had said. "The virus can be carried in from anywhere."

Infected livestock had been shot and their carcases incinerated.

And Bill Henderson could still not prevent himself throwing a relieved glance over the site of a neighbouring farm's mass cremation each time he drove past.

The Ministry's first all-industry briefing was in London. An oval table with scores of seats was ringed by an equal number of agitated representatives who had to stand.

A section head who'd drawn the short straw sat centre top. He was flanked by the Chief Vet, Gethryn, and other senior advisors. Note takers had fanned out either side.

"We have seven confirmed cases," confirmed Section Head.

The groan that greeted this announcement was unsettling.

A side door opened. A clerk handed Chief Vet a note.

"We now have eleven. Their distribution continues to be both wide and unusual. The national movement restrictions imposed two days ago cannot be relaxed."

That meant FMD susceptible animals – sheep, pigs or cattle – could not be moved off the farm where they currently stood.

"I have 250 in-lamb ewes wintering in the Welsh Borders," barked a farmer. "They'll run out of feed if they're not back home in two weeks."

"Mine are in Lincolnshire. They can't lamb on their own," growled another.

Note takers shuffled uneasily. Those not used to noisy breaches of Whitehall protocol coughed.

A deep, disturbed, rural murmur spread. Cash flow would freeze. Tens of thousands of finishing animals would lose value at the same time as the cost of keeping them increased.

"We already know the circumstances surrounding this outbreak are exceptional," said Section Head. "Many more cases are anticipated and all susceptible animals on these premises will be slaughtered as soon as infection is confirmed."

He looked down the room.

"Many more cases.

"Over an unusually wide area.

"We will meet again at this time next week."

Ben was driving cross-country to catch an early train when he saw a red glow. An infected farm was being cleaned out.

The scene was mediaeval. Dozens of animals were being burned on a railway sleeper funeral pyre. He could see heads and legs silhouetted in the flames. More carcases waited to be incinerated. Firelight flickered on busy human shadows. It was a sight, he knew, would soon be repeated many times elsewhere.

A wagon loaded with yet more railway sleepers, its headlights questing, was turning into the farm gate.

"There are thirty-eight confirmed cases," Section Head told his next all-industry meeting.

"Mainly down the west side of the country. Sheep farms in Devon, Wales, Cumbria and South-West Scotland account for most."

The room was just as crowded. Its occupants more unsettled than before.

Stock from some farms could be sold on licence for immediate home consumption but the export of meat to EU countries had been banned.

And susceptible animals on farms that shared boundaries with an infected holding were being compulsorily slaughtered too.

Families were stunned. They'd heard their animals being shot. Their busy farmyards had been emptied. Buildings echoed. Husbandry routines had been abandoned because there was nothing left to keep. Contractors hired by the Ministry were disinfecting every crack and cranny. Eyes watered and the buildings stank. When they too moved on the silence was deafening.

And if neighbours who still had stock saw new bonfire smoke, they winced.

"One hundred and twenty-six cases," said Section Head a week later. "The Royal Army Veterinary Corps has been called in to help MAFF vets keep pace with slaughter."

The crack of captive bolt pistols was unrelenting. Elimination of the virus could not be compromised. If a farm was infected, or its fields touched one that was, no animal was spared.

Some farms complained their stock had gone down because cremation ash and other clean-up debris from diseased neighbours had been blown in.

"It's desperate," said Gethryn. "The pigs found in Kent came off a farm where contagion may have festered for weeks. We are working on the theory that virus carried from them to nearby sheep which were put, with no indications of sickness, through a crowded auction market attended by purchasers who'd come in from just about everywhere under the sun. Circumstances could hardly have been more unfavourable. We've still to discover the depth of the damage but fear the worst. Confirmed cases will soon reach five hundred and we expect many more."

"What was the original source?"

"Most likely untreated swill. Possibly from a restaurant. We're running out of railway sleepers. The army has been called out to dig mass graves. Downing Street's directly involved and new control policies are being thrashed out in Cabinet Briefing Room "A". COBRA."

It was a resonant name.

"What can you tell me?"

Neither Henderson, nor Jim, or the Kerrs would let visitors onto their farms. Milk collection lorries, the only outsiders allowed in, were soaked in disinfectant and their drivers ordered to stay in their cabs. Alice shopped for each household and dropped their groceries at the gate.

"Siege mentality dominates. Everyone's fed up but no one sensible wants to risk losing their stock. Most farms accept they are in it for the long term. And there may be a black market for infected tongues."

"We've heard that too."

"Why would anyone do that?" said Jim over the phone.

"There'll always be chancers. People with poor quality stock, or failing businesses, keen to grab a windfall compensation cheque."

"They should be strung up by their balls," said Jim.

The radio had just told him that every sheep within three kilometres of an infected farm would have to be killed as well.

Ben told Kit and Pita not to hurry with their preparations.

"We're in lockdown. Some footpaths have been closed. Most rural attractions have shut. Tourism has collapsed. Our General Election's been put back until June and Livinton's not far from the worst of the trouble. They won't risk infecting their own stock and they'll want to look after their neighbours as well. You may have to wait a year."

"OK," said Kit. "We'll take our time and do it properly."

"How're things going?"

"There's lots of excitement and more volunteers than we need."

Henderson was terse.

"Davy Reed's found six sheep's tongues in one of his roadside water troughs. He could see the blisters."

"Where are they now?"

"Same place. Told him not to touch them and call a vet."

"We're looking at our biggest domestic upheaval since the war," said Gethryn. "The only good news is that the outbreak may have peaked."

"A fortnight ago we confirmed fifty cases in one day but we haven't topped that since."

"What's the national total?" asked Ben.

"More than nine hundred so far. We daren't relax our grip."

The standstill on stock movement began to make problems of its own. Some farms ran short of forage, and cattle especially began to starve.

A Livestock Welfare Disposal Scheme was introduced. Animals on overstocked farms that were still under restriction could be surrendered then killed. Owners were compensated and the payments were attractive because valuations had improved.

"Someone must be feeling sorry for us," said Edward Kerr.

That might have been true, but the official view was that because sheep and cattle numbers had been thinned dramatically, replacements were already scarce. Which meant that when farms that had been cleaned out began to re-stock, the price of incoming animals would rocket.

The Chancellor of the Exchequer was worried. His officials had estimated the cost of controlling the epidemic could top £3 billion with perhaps £1 billion spent on slaughter compensation alone.

"Schemes encourage schemers," said Gethryn. "I've no doubt some welfare cases are genuine but I'm equally certain some farms are grabbing a chance to unload poor quality stock at prices they would once have dreamed of."

The deliberate import of infection through black market tongues was another worry. There were reports of fights if a farmer was suspected of deliberately contaminating his own holding and raising the risk for others.

"We'll never get to the bottom of it," said Gethryn. "Some will think an FMD clear out, then a cheque, is the equivalent of early retirement. Others could see it as way of being paid to drop unprofitable stock farming and a chance to move into something else?"

Ben thought Britain's cheap food policy was the ultimate culprit because sheep and cattle were almost always sold for less than it cost to produce them. Subsidy payments had been installed to compensate for these low prices but their one-size-fits-all demands were clumsy and introduced unnecessary expense of their own.

The last of 2,026 cases was confirmed that autumn.

More than 10,000 farms had been slaughtered out.

More than six million animals had been destroyed.

Total cost, including lost income in tourist areas, had topped £8 billion.

The bill for welfare disposal alone had been £200 million.

"The silence was the worst thing," said one farmer.

His subdued family described the emptiness of their once bustling holding as "creepy".

"We couldn't wait to re-stock and get some life back on the place," he added.

Whitehall set out to make the UK's defence against FMD more effective.

The interim ban imposed on swill feeding was confirmed as permanent.

And a six-day, single holding, standstill to curb the swirl of national livestock movement was imposed on all farms that managed sheep, pigs, or cattle.

Nothing could be moved off a farm until almost a week after the last incoming animal had moved on.

Vets and civil servants had pressed for a 14-day standstill. But weary farmers insisted it would make livestock management too difficult because it would freeze commercial exchange too long.

It was hoped the shorter suspension would still give vets time to trace infection spread, and then make health checks, if another emergency erupted.

"You've got the all-clear," Ben told Kit.

"Livinton and everyone else have given next May's opening ceremony the green light. The delay will work to our advantage. Last spring the country was under siege. This year there'll be optimism and relief. Visitors will be hungry for entertainment and desperate to get out. You couldn't be arriving at a better time."

He rang his fellow Disciples.

"They didn't shoot you as well?" said Farid.

"You'll be pleased to have got that behind you," said Chris.

And outlined his Livinton plan.

"Real live Pagambans?" said Daryl.

"Spears and feathers?" said Maggie. "It can't go wrong."

He told them he'd be in touch after Christmas.

"Welcome back," said Judy.

She'd spent summer watching her sons rowing and had seen Aaron's eight win a final at Henley.

He crewed for August College in London and like his former PE Teacher was fanatic.

Abel was going to university in London too. He had set his sights on being the Princes College stroke.

They were middle class, Ben reflected. Very Crown Lane.

He'd shown them where Scott and Alice had lived on Bentcross.

"A slice of a house," Aaron had said when the reality of the accommodation offered by a terraced two-up two-down had sunk in.

Abel had paced out its width.

"It's less than half our kitchen."

He'd told them he and Catherine had shared a double bed with a bolster down the middle while Tom sang to himself in a nearby cot but wasn't sure they believed him.

CHAPTER 21

"I'd promised to look after someone so I did."

He was with the Pagambans when their bus pulled up at Livinton Hall in a churn of excitement and with a mountain of luggage.

He'd met them at Heathrow and was pleased he had because everyone had been nervous.

Kobe and Matrissia were the minders.

Good choices, he thought. The Ongil's no-nonsense tough guy and a headman's wife with embedded authority.

"How'd selection go?" he'd asked Kit.

"They just about picked themselves. We asked for volunteers then concentrated on those from the same age group who'd been at school together."

They'd had three days in London, as guests of the Pagamban High Commission which had paid their airfare, and had shed jetlag during a boat trip down the Thames and visits to Westminster, Windsor Castle and The Tower.

"Dormitories first," said Jonathon, leading them upstairs. "Chose your bed, and cupboard space, then come down for lunch."

Kobe led off the young men and Matrissia the young women. When they saw their beds had been arranged in a circle there was instant approving chatter.

"They're here," he told the Disciples. "We need all the publicity we can get. The High Commission took photos when they were in London."

He gave an email address and number.

"It'll send anything you order. Come up here for a preview or fresh pictures anytime you like.

"I'm sending press releases to both nationals and regionals. Press, radio and TV.

"This is the line."

"Jonathon Beltingham-Norris-d'Antille lives in a fortress his family has held for generations but it must be repaired before it falls around his ears. The bills will be huge so he must raise money.

Crispin, his son and heir, is married to my sister which is why I'm trying to help.

He and his father will be opening new visitor attractions at Livinton Hall on the first Saturday in May.

They're beating a big publicity drum and my son, Doctor Kit Kunjin Robson, who is a Pagamban, from the Ongil clan, is helping my sister, his aunt and mother of his cousins, to rescue her husband's family seat.

With him are twenty-six of his Ongil clansman who have come to help as well.

They will be staging traditional dances, not yet seen in Britain, in the main arena each afternoon for two weeks.

It's British heritage in reverse.

The opposite to pith helmeted derring-do through darkest Africa or wide Indian plains.

On this occasion the infamously fierce, spear carrying men of Pagamba, and its handsome young women, have gathered at Livinton to help their cash-poor, aristocratic British relatives, continue to live in their crumbling ancestral home."

"What will the dancers be wearing?" asked Maggie.

"Traditional costume."

"What will the women be wearing?" asked Chris.

"Traditional costume"

"What does that mean?" asked Daryl.

"Feather head dresses, grass skirts and bare chests."

"They'll change their minds," said Farid.

"Don't think so. They've said it's their heritage and that's how it's going to be."

They had, too.

Matrissia had told them British people might feel uncomfortable if they showed their breasts.

Some could tut-tut, she said, even complain.

"What about?" said Kimbil.

Her clan sisters frowned.

"Ben says some silly men might shout rude things," said Matrissia.

The Pagambans were annoyed. Some shook their heads. One stamped her foot. Another hissed. An exhalation of derision forced between tongue and teeth.

"No T-shirt for me," said Kundup. "I'm not covering up."

"I'm proud of my breasts. They'll never look better," said Waura.

"We are Ongil," they told Matrissia. "These are our customs. We always dance bare chested. We will do it our way."

Ben, Kit, Kobe and Matrissia were sitting together.

They had agreed the troupe would dance twice daily.

But the opening ceremony was a one-off. They would have to put together something special.

The squad had squirmed with excitement when they heard The Top Princess would be watching.

Ben was surprised as well. Jonathon must have more influence up there, at the hierarchical summit, than he had thought.

Kobe was still annoyed.

"What for silly people like get cross with Ongil girl?"

Mattrissia agreed.

"I'd give them something to tut-tut about."

She shook her shoulders.

Her breasts quivered under her blouse.

Kobe laughed.

"That good. When drum make boom girl make jiggle."

Matrissia slapped her thigh.

"Many booms. Many jiggles."

Ben and Catherine rode through Livinton Hall's main gate together.

They wore matching hacking jackets, were mounted on Captain and Gunner, and were holding Pagamban flags.

Kit, in traditional dress, followed on foot. Bird of Paradise plumes danced on his head, the multi-leafed bustle over his backside rustled, his legs were bare to the waist, and a long, woven, loin cover flapped against his ankles. The spear he carried in shoulder-arms position was nine feet long. It was a traditional Ongil butang with a thin, two-feet blade and four spikes beneath it that could tear out an eye, or rip out muscle, as it passed.

Six young Ongil men walked, line across, behind him. They too wore traditional costume and they each carried a hand drum.

Applause lifted when the girls filed out. They had crowned themselves with long red feathers, their grass skirts flowed, and strings of shell hung from their necks.

They walked line of six on each side of the road. A second group of six men, also carrying drums, and walking line across, fell in behind.

Last place in the column was Kobe's. He too was carrying a butang spear.

He rolled his eyes at the crowd lining the road and shook it.

Camera shutters clicked, there was laughter, and he was encouraged to do it again.

Stall holders, there to sell food or ice cream, clapped as well.

The parade ground was ringed with people. Its grandstand was packed.

Catherine and Ben, flags high, led the Ongils in.

Jonathon, in a reproduction of the MacGregor tartan a distant grandfather had worn during the 1715 Jacobite rebellion, marched through, and bowed when he reached the stand.

"Welcome to Livinton Hall Your Royal Highness."

The Top Princess told everyone she was pleased the FMD epidemic was over, welcomed the Pagambans to Britain, declared the Livinton Estate and its many attractions open to visitors, and sat down.

The hand drums boomed once. The girls bowed to the stand. They boomed again. The girls skipped sideways so they were facing the crowd and bowed again.

Another boom. The girls shook their shoulders and jumped sideways. Boom. They shook their shoulders and jumped back. There was more applause.

The Top Princess stepped down. She shook hands with Jonathon, Ben and Catherine then patted Gunner's neck.

"What a grand old man."

After she'd shaken hands with Kit she turned to her security guards.

"I'm going to meet those plucky gels. If you suggest otherwise I'll tell you to sod orf."

They surrounded her, skirts shiffing, after they'd shaken her hand.

They answered her questions together and laughed at the same time.

Farid's camera was working hard. Other newspaper photographers were busy.

Maggie's TV unit zoomed in as well. ,

The red headdresses shook their shoulders even more enthusiastically when they about turned.

They repeated it every tenth pace as the Pagambans filed out.

A Tannoy crackled.

"And after that what comes next?"

"My goodness…what have we here?"

The Morvale Hunt, riders in pink, and hounds curious, trotted in to fresh applause.

Hunstman gathered his reins, put his horn to his lips, and tooted follow on as he cantered the perimeter.

When the whipper-in had gathered hounds in the centre of the ring children were invited to pat them.

A line of haltered British Longhorn cattle and heavy horses pulling a selection of drays and carts waited their turn.

"We'd better get up to the house," Jonathon told Hortense. "Mustn't keep The Top Princess waiting."

The girls were ready to show her round.

"Seen enough big houses to last a lifetime," she said. "Let's sit in the kitchen."

"We'd like that," said Kundup.

"Bang on, young lady. Lead the way."

***

"I see Ben every time I look at you," Julie told Kit.

They were on the lawn at Crown House where Judy had arranged a gathering.

"Everyone," she'd said. "Ongil, Robson, Henderson, Johnston and Clark."

"So do I," said Hattie.

She called Aaron and Abel over.

"Stand next to Kit," she ordered as only an elder sister can.

"Are any of Hilda's family here?"

"Oh yes," said Kit. "I'll get my cousins."

He came back with Kundup, Waura, Anton and Bau.

"Right," said Julie. "Let's get Ben."

Judy and Matrissia had found a quiet corner.

"What was she like?"

"Determined. Once she'd decided she wanted to live with him he didn't stand a chance."

"He never did take the lead," said Judy.

"Dad," said Aaron. "We've been talking to Kobe."

He pretended to groan.

"He say what thing?"

"Lots of things," said Abel. "He's funny."

They looked at each other.

"What did you do with your shotgun when you were ambushed at Kwishebe?"

He hadn't told anyone and he was not going to tell them.

"I'd promised to look after someone so I did."

He sat on the bank beneath the oak trees because he was unsettled.

Waura looked just like the Hilda who had followed him when he set off with Diman for Kwinika.

His British sons' question had revived memories he'd thought long gone.

And he liked Kit. They got on well. There would be a gap in his life when he returned home.

Judy was unaffected. He watched her orchestrating her garden party with typical assurance. She was enjoying herself.

He rarely thought about Hilda but was sure he would still be with her, and Kit, in Pagamba if she was alive.

Would his life have been better than it was now?

Who could tell? Who indeed.

However, it would, without doubt, have been different.

Pagamba was a blank canvas while Britain was cramped and there was much less room to move.

He was happier than he had thought he could ever be when he had returned alone to Whiteside.

He had told no one that even now it could feel strange to be living on Crown Lane.

Many said he was lucky. That he'd enjoyed an unusual adventure then landed on his feet like a cat.

But life with Judy had kicked off only because Charles then Hilda had died.

And he knew without equivocation there was nothing remotely fortunate about that.

End